Praise for
GARGOYLE SAFARI

"In *Gargoyle Safari*, Marano not only molds language—shifting style with the subgenre and influences of each story—but conjures it with the ease of some prose-wizard. Each tale carries its own distinct flavor, its own inventive approach, and a wild imagination that never strays into inaccessibility. The weirdness runs just deep enough to lend an umami-rich undertone, the kind that invites you to peel back the surface and discover what lurks underneath. *Gargoyle Safari* is one of the best collections I've read in years." —C. F. Page, author of *Native Fear* and *The Swallowed Town*

"Luciano Marano writes horror like an undercover reporter from the margins of a haunted world in mid-collapse. With a shrewd eye for detail, square-jawed prose, and the occasional fleck of gold in a pitch-black heart, *Gargoyle Safari's* mad ones and monsters won't let readers escape." —Gordon B. White, finalist for the Shirley Jackson and Bram Stoker Awards

"Marano's range is astonishing. Here is an author who has steeped himself in life and literature, and who fashions his fictions into beautiful palimpsests that reveal both the underlayer of inspiration as well as the glowing epidermis that is his unique vision and voice." —C.M. Muller (from his introduction)

GARGOYLE SAFARI

a collection of stories by
LUCIANO MARANO

JOURNALSTONE
YOUR LINK TO ARTIST TALENT

This is a work of fiction. All of the characters, names, incidents, organizations, and dialogue in this novel are either the products of the author's imagination or are used fictitiously.

The views expressed in this work are solely those of the authors and do not necessarily reflect the views of the publisher, and the publisher hereby disclaims any responsibility for them.

ISBN: 978-1-68510-176-3 (trade paper)
ISBN: 978-1-68510-177-0 (ebook)
Library of Congress Catalog Number: 2026933533

First printing edition: February 20, 2026
Published by JournalStone Publishing in the United States of America.
Cover Artwork and Design: Serafine Hollowood
Edited by Sean Leonard
Proofreading and Cover/Interior Layout by Scarlett R. Algee

JournalStone Publishing
1400 North Wood Rd.
Murphysboro, IL 62966

JournalStone books may be ordered through booksellers or by contacting:
JournalStone | www.journalstone.com

With the exception of one story, which has its own separate dedication, this book is for You—whoever You are, however You found it, no matter how much of it You ultimately decide to finish and whether You like it or not. After all, none of this matters if nobody reads.

"Writing isn't about making money, getting famous, getting dates, getting laid, or making friends. In the end, it's about enriching the lives of those who will read your work, and enriching your own life, as well."
—Stephen King, "On Writing: A Memoir of the Craft"

CONTENTS

INTRODUCTION

Three years ago, when I was refashioning my annual anthology series *Nightscript* into a quarterly now known as *Chthonic Matter*, I spent months combing through submissions, seeking stories to incorporate into this new incarnation of "strange and darksome" tales, as well as *the story* that would stand as its thoughtful, creepy opener.

That submission turned out to be "Love is a Ghost You See with Your Heart," the title of which immediately lit my imagination. But it was the story that followed that truly won me over. It is a brilliantly constructed tale of haunters and the haunted, as well as an intriguing treatise on the writerly life. To wit: *There are no such things as ghosts, probably. But I actually think writers are like ghosts to the people who love us and live with us — often more presence than present.*

And while that particular piece provides the closer to this collection, it seems strangely appropriate that the opening "attraction" is the equally powerful "The Mythologization of Tymber Prescott in Five Selected Photos," which originally appeared in the eighth and final edition of *Nightscript*. Here again we have another uniquely constructed tale, only this time Marano turns his clever and prescient vision on the ills of social media.

The strength of this collection — this safari of the strange — lies in its diverse offerings. From the quite horror of "Love is a Ghost You See with Your Heart," to the splatterpunk stylings of "'Till the Road Runs Out"; from the King-inspired "Struggle As You Will to Rise," to the Wagnerian (as in Karl Edward Wagner) "My Eyes Are Closed to Your Light," Marano's range is astonishing. Here is an author who has steeped himself in life and literature, and who fashions his fictions into beautiful palimpsests that reveal both the underlayer of inspiration as well as the glowing epidermis that is his unique vision and voice.

Consider this barker-brief intro your ticket to the safari. Turn the page, good reader — you're guaranteed to enjoy this singular show.

C.M. Muller

GARGOYLE SAFARI

The Mythologization of Tymber Prescott in Five Selected Photos

It helps that she's dead now, because we never thought of her as a real person anyway. She was an aspiration, the avatar of something we wanted or wanted to be. An attractive algorithm with a pretty face and keen sense of style, designed to be irresistible and sell us stuff. She was basically a brand, like any other. At least we no longer have to feel conflicted about what happened to her—the few of us who did, that is.

Her objectification was an achievement of sorts. She was everything to everyone, inscrutable but endlessly appealing. Mona Lisa in fair trade fashion. The girl next door with eyes full of unspoken promises, more followers than the Dalai Lama, and liked by absolutely everyone.

A true influencer, she made it easier for us with every post.

Tymber Prescott always looked good. She knew exactly what she wanted, was happier than we could ever understand. She was certainly not alive in the same way as lesser humans like us—people with desperate hopes and bitter disappointments, shame, regret, and secret thoughts we could never share.

Her perfection haunted us.

Her destruction obsessed us.

Now, her feed fascinates us for very different reasons.

————

Influence: the capacity to have an effect on the character, development, or behavior of someone or something; or the effect itself.

————

1. Cottagecore Cutie

Vibrant in a pink thermal shirt and white overalls against the crumbling interior of a ruined cabin, it was exactly this sense of personality—cute, cocky, perfectly posed—that shot Tymber from zero to more than 60,000 followers on the app in her first year alone.

Hands jammed into pockets, blonde hair flowing from beneath a black watch cap, Tymber laughs at us, rocking back playfully on her heels. She is incongruously at ease in such a place. You want to warn her away. It somehow doesn't feel right that she should be there, that anybody should. How much of that reaction is due to our knowledge of subsequent events is impossible to say. Still, the place is eerie.

Scorch marks on the splintered wall behind her seem less than random, an unsettling pattern of darker blacks beneath the char of some long ago fire. A stain, or perhaps a weirdly intricate growth of mold, sends seeking tendrils upward from the ground beneath Tymber's tan boots. A moldering blanket of leaves and bristling patches of brown grass. Here and there, small round beads of shiny black stone glint in the weak rays of light coming through what we imagine are holes in whatever remains of the sagging structure's roof. High on the wall, underneath the mold, a vague design of scratches can be seen. Curling lines within a circle, seemingly too deliberate to be the work of weather or wildlife.

Likely taken by Oliver Perkins, noted lifestyle photographer, the picture is the last of several Tymber posted from a weekend trip to a rural section of the Olympic Peninsula, where she and other models, influencers, and photographers from the Seattle area rented a house for a collaborative working weekend.

Investigators subsequently ascertained Tymber and Oliver went for a walk around noon and returned later than expected, nearly causing the group to miss their intended ferry back to the city. Others in the party said the pair were behaving strangely when they got back; "like they were high or something," said one witness. In the case of Oliver, known to be a regular drinker and frequent user of drugs, this was not unusual. Tymber, however, did not often imbibe, and at least one witness expressed concern for her.

Searches of the area conducted after Tymber's death located no cabin. Oliver, of course, could not be asked about the image, as he was found dead just two weeks after the trip. Authorities assert he fell and struck his head in the kitchen of his Ballard apartment and bled to death while intoxicated by a combination of codeine and alcohol.

Initial evidence seemed to suggest another person was present at the time, but the investigation was ultimately inconclusive.

---

2. Sweaty & Ready

Tymber's athleticism was often a secondary aspect of her influencer persona. However, seeing her in workout clothes and holding a kettlebell, muscles flexed, we are reminded she initially rose to fame as a fitness model.

Wearing gray tights, white sneakers, and a black sports bra, Tymber's hair is pulled loosely back in a playful pink band. She is standing beside a wall of windows in a large room with padded floors. The light is warm and clear. She is turned partially away from us, looking over her shoulder with a mysterious smile that is part challenge, part invitation. She wears no makeup or jewelry beyond a small gold stud in the visible ear. She is lightly sweating, as if having just completed a warmup, she is ready to begin exercising in earnest.

On the skin of her shoulder is an area of discoloration. It might be a bruise, though it's almost perfectly symmetrical. The outline of the shape is more prominent, easier to spot. And within the circle are faint lines which seem to curl inward as if part of an intricate design.

Her eyes, previously a startlingly light green, appear different now, darker. A shade of brown so deep as to be almost black.

---

3. #nothappy

Her expression is difficult to decipher. Tymber sits on the floor just inside a pair of slim white doors, one open to reveal a small balcony rimmed by ornate blue ironwork outside. The light is dull and gray, threatening rain. She sits on a plush rug in faded jeans and a billowy yellow sweater. Her legs are not fully visible. The nails on the fingers we can see, on the hand not holding her phone, are unpainted, though the skin beneath each is lightly blue.

Again, she wears no makeup. The dark circles beneath her eyes are obvious. She is smiling, but it has the feel of habit rather than true expression. Despite the apparent chill of the day and the open door, there is a thin sheen of sweat on Tymber's forehead. It is not difficult to imagine she will soon begin to cry. The image has the feel of a haphazard selfie more than staged photograph meant for posting. And yet, post it she did, without hashtags or explanation.

The location of the room in which the picture was taken remains unknown. When asked later, Tymber's friends and associates were unable, or unwilling, to provide authorities with any additional information.

In the wake of this post, and several likewise melancholic and ambiguous selfies shared shortly after, Tymber's number of followers leapt astronomically.

---

4. The Infamous Mirror Image

Easily the most famous of her series of bizarre selfies, this picture is unquestionably more responsible than any other for the disturbing rumors that surround the influencer's sudden grisly and mysterious death just six days after it was posted.

She'd been avoiding friends, investigators later ascertained. She hadn't been seen in public for weeks. Essentially, Tymber did not exist beyond her increasingly strange postings to various social media platforms.

Here, Tymber leans forward, face close to the bathroom mirror. The hand of her raised arm is out of frame, likely braced against the wall, while the other holds a phone near her shoulder, lens forward. Though shirtless, Tymber's hair, wild and tangled, clearly unwashed, is long enough to obscure her breasts. She is terribly pale, and looks even more so against the uniformly white tile of the bathroom. Despite the light source above the unseen mirror, her eyes appear entirely black.

There is a trickle of what may be blood coming down Tymber's forehead from somewhere within her hair, though the viscous liquid seems too thick and dark. She is very thin, with much of the lean muscle on display in previous photos seemingly wasted away. On her concave belly and boney hips can be seen a forest of harsh red scratches, the sort which may have been inflicted by the claws of a large cat or perhaps her own fingernails—those we can see have grown long and ragged. The waistband and visible portion of her light blue briefs look soiled.

Most disturbing of all, however, is her expression. Tymber's mouth hangs open, her discolored tongue lolling to one side, much longer than it should be. Milky drool slicks her chin. And although the edges of her cracked and bleeding lips are pulled slightly upward, as if in a smile, the young woman appears at the same time to be screaming. Looking back now, one cannot help but wonder if she was perhaps calling for help.

The image has received more likes and comments than any other Tymber ever posted. It has been shared countless times and remains a popular meme.

---

5. #whoiswithme?

Her feet, bare and dirty. The last photo posted to Tymber's feed, barely two hours before she was found dead. One imagines she was sitting with her knees up and apart, soles pressed nearly together.

Her skin is cut, deeply in places, and blood flows through the frosting of filth smeared across her feet. Dark blue veins bulge in small patches on her ankles and the portion of her calves we can see. Her toenails are black. Several have split apart and blood oozes from the ravaged tips of her toes. A small shard of glass can be seen, distractingly shiny amidst so much darkness, piercing Tymber's left heel.

She had clearly been walking without shoes, but for how long? And where? What is the meaning of her final hashstag? A siren call to would-be imitators? Encouragement to follow in the troubled icon's suicidal footsteps? Or is it simply the honest and desperate final question posed by a terrified young woman who was—or at least believed she was—in the thrall of some inexplicable influence?

These are just a few of the many questions that plague those who seek answers to the question of what truly happened to Tymber Prescott.

According to law enforcement, not long after posting the image, the 24-year-old influencer leapt to her death from the top floor of a commercial parking structure in Seattle's downtown business district.

She has since been the focus of several investigations, both written features and broadcast TV specials alike, along with countless YouTube videos done with widely varying levels of respect and production quality.

To this day, there are those who insist Tymber committed suicide while under the control of a supernatural force. Others argue it was true demonic possession, using her story to warn non-believers of the dangers of godless glory and vapid idolatry.

Most balk at such notions, however, maintaining Tymber was simply the victim of an undiagnosed, but decidedly non-supernatural, mental illness, nothing more.

Admittedly, members of the latter camp struggle to explain the state of her apartment.

In Tymber's home, police allegedly found extensive writings carved into the walls, written in numerous languages, none of them English and not one of which Tymber was known to speak. Also, several advanced mathematical equations were scrawled in human blood and excrement on her living room floor, apparently solved. Experts remain in disagreement as to the technical accuracy of her solutions, the math being of a reportedly highly experimental and theoretical variety, perhaps unprovable. But none of them can explain how a C-average student who hadn't completed a single hour of college instruction could manage as much as she did.

And rumors persist of more macabre findings in the apartment—bottles filled with urine; dozens of watches, all of them broken; a mound of dead birds in one closet; bones that appeared to have been gnawed; and, perhaps most disturbing of all, several articles of shredded children's clothing.

No officials involved with the case have cooperated with outside investigators or journalists. Several, in fact, have died premature and mysterious deaths themselves, a fact which only strengthens the resolve of those insisting the ultimate cause of Tymber's condition to be supernatural.

Meanwhile, Tymber herself lives on after death, in a way.

Ascendancy: occupation of a position of great power, dominance, or absolute influence.

———~~~———

Her photos are a ubiquitous presence on social media. She remains a popular choice for those seeking a Halloween costume both sexy and scary. The strange symbol on her shoulder is a tattoo favored by rising influencers and celebrity personalities. Her likeness has even been found painted on buildings in various cities around the world. A kind of new secular saint, Tymber's visage seems to mark scenes of similar, likewise unexplained, suicides. Of which, for whatever reason, there are many of late. And more happening all the time.

North American government health officials have persistently stopped short of calling the recent spike of suicides among young people an epidemic. Tech company representatives continue to be reticent to discuss the appearance among posts made by the deceased including Tymber's now-infamous hashtag—#whoiswithme? Such posts are typically flagged, if not removed, by company moderators, though critics and parent groups insist such action to be an insufficient response. Industry experts are in disagreement as to the connection, if any, between the proliferation of such content and national suicide trends. And free speech advocates rush to decry such censorship as both unnecessary and unethical.

The debate rages on.

Meanwhile, independent research and multiple surveys conducted by mental health advocacy groups in the United States and Canada claim an indisputable correlation between these otherwise unexplained deaths and posts containing the image and/or famous last words of Tymber Prescott.

Of course, such evidence in no way proves those deaths are the result of a widening instance of some sort of mass possession, the work of supernatural or demonic forces, as many claim (some religious groups have gone so far as to encourage their members to avoid the internet altogether). But neither does it establish the existence of a lethal copycat craze among impressionable young people, a kind of "lethal viral challenge" as mainstream media outlets and some prominent psychologists insist.

All that's certain is the continuing presence of Tymber Prescott, inscrutable and enigmatic as ever. Her story is somehow aspirational and simultaneously cautionary. What exactly about this figure continues to resonate with so many is a mystery.

Only her influence is beyond question.

Gargoyle Safari

Somebody got Mammon two nights ago with a hammer. They tossed pieces of him off the roof of the old credit union. An especially large chunk hit a woman out for a predawn run and cracked her skull in half.

Unbelievable, I thought. What kind of lunatic goes jogging in that neighborhood? Had my hometown really changed so much?

Mammon was the third grotesque to be destroyed in as many months, but this was the first person to get hurt in the process. Guerrilla vandals performing unsanctioned midnight demolitions of stone monsters was one thing. The loss of a single tax-paying citizen—one registered to vote, no less—that couldn't be tolerated. I'd been gone for nearly a decade, but the city's priorities were the same apparently.

Crime was on the rise, a sudden and otherwise inexplicable spike in shoplifting, burglaries, assaults. An election loomed on the not-too-distant horizon. The gargoyle safari was probably a coincidence. But then again, maybe not.

The city council's offer found me on the other side of the world, slogging through a boring corporate divination gig, and promised more cash than I could afford to turn down. Thankfully, they didn't bother appealing to my nonexistent sense of civic duty and were smart enough not to mention my father or Chase Grayson. I read their report, consulted the runes, then checked my bank balance. Those sad numbers were the only sign I really needed.

Still, I hesitated.

Something in the ether, maybe? Ominous portents vying for my attention. It could have been an instinctive reaction to the idea of going home again, or trusting the council, even a little. I was not without options, I reminded myself, throwing clothes into a suitcase. I was an intelligent young woman with extremely marketable skills, after all. Nothing said this had to be my problem, right?

Yeah, right.

I loved puzzles. But the campaign of architectural assassinations posed, to me, the more interesting mystery. Did the statues honor the monsters they depicted or serve as warnings against such evils? Did the city's gargoyles offer protection from malicious influences or simply placate them?

And, most intriguingly, what would happen if they were suddenly all gone?

Part of me wanted to know. Part of me thought the city deserved to find out how bad things could really get. But another slightly larger part wanted to pay my father's hospital bills and not starve in the process. So I packed my crystals and silver, candles and chalk, and like a good prodigal witch booked a seat in row 13 on the next flight home.

There weren't many monsters left to begin with.

Nobody knew the exact number, but most of the city's gargoyles had been demolished along with the antiquated buildings on which they'd perched. Victims of longtime systemic neglect, then sudden explosive urban renewal. Bested by the likes of Neiman Marcus and Cartier, a slew of boutique grocery stores, gastropubs, and chic condos, the city's ancient mason menagerie were sacrifices eagerly laid upon the altars of progress and convenience.

Soon we'd have nothing left to fear but each other.

The old fairy tales had been thoroughly Disneyfied long ago. Movie franchises turned fiends like Leatherface, Freddy, and Jason into icons whose likenesses we plastered on shirts and inked into our skin. We made rock stars of serial killers. Baphomet was a keychain, Cthulhu a plush toy. And *Vote for Satan* graced a million bumper stickers (*Why settle for the lesser evil?*). Now the dwindling population of gargoyles, that already-threatened stone subspecies of monster, was short even more specimens.

The night I returned, a winged lion atop the train station was reduced to rubble. Two days later, at an elegant Victorian apartment building, somebody destroyed Asmodeus. I visited the crime scenes, stood on the vacant ledges and empty rooftops, drew chalk circles and broke out my quartz pendant. I poured shallow pools of blessed water, looked deeply and perceived...my own reflection.

Sorry, folks, nothing to *scry* here.

Prices and the unemployment rate both went up.

Astaroth was beheaded above the university library's entryway.

And all the while, society frayed a bit more. Nothing drastic at first, no need to activate the national guard or declare an emergency. But it occupied local authorities enough so that nobody was available to watch over potential non-human victims. And it kept the press from caring too much about the ongoing gargoyle genocide.

I sensed something insidious in the air, a kind of mounting communal dread, as I wandered, trying to divine hints of the vandal. The city was familiar to me, but also strange. It wasn't merely the development and construction which had occurred in my absence. Little things seemed *wrong* somehow, as if seen through the haze of exhaustion. Everyone felt it, I think. Things were getting worse, it was undeniable, but nobody could articulate the impression or say exactly why.

And life went on, regardless.

People walked quickly with heads down and earbuds in; that is, when they left their homes at all. The cacophony of gunfire and sirens became commonplace. Traffic congestion made streets impassable and filled the air with noxious fumes. Broken windows and hateful graffiti spread across the city like sores on the flesh of a plague victim.

But life still went on, as always.

If the world ends gradually enough, turns out most people won't notice.

A pair of harpies were obliterated, wings and claws left in a pile among other less identifiable pieces. A woman drove her SUV through a farmers market, mowing people down and laughing hysterically while the stereo blared Boys II Men's "End of the Road." There were protests, some of which nearly became riots. All of them earned disproportionately forceful responses from the police.

I adopted nondescript glamours to explore the darker streets, held one séance after another, read the entrails of a dozen chickens. Urgent emails from the city council piled up in my inbox, unopened.

The utter lack of ethereal evidence meant the vandal was somebody who knew their stuff. A person uninitiated in the ways of magic couldn't help but leave a trace of themselves behind. It narrowed my list of suspects, but made each one all the more dangerous.

An especially old gargoyle, which sat on the historic clocktower in Market Square since time immemorial, was destroyed.

I walked past half-naked lunatics screwing behind mounting piles of uncollected garbage. Clusters of tents and sleeping bags sprouted on the sidewalks, huddled forms shifting listlessly inside. Addicts collapsed and died on the street as I stalked past, pendant dangling from one hand, the other always ready to fling a hex or paralysis spell.

A young security guard, having evidentially stumbled upon the vandal in action, got himself tossed off the 16th story of Atlantic Tower, along with broken pieces of the archangel Uriel.

Some very angry man in a crowded supermarket opened fire with an assault rifle.

Seeing no other recourse, I made my way to Canal Street. A portion of the city as yet untouched by the malaise, but only because it was always fairly rough. A token effort at renewal had begun even there, but it was pitiful. Like putting makeup on a corpse already starting to decompose.

Marcello Tumminelli lounged on a bench in one of the scraggly lots that passed for a park in that neighborhood, brown paper bag between his legs, wearing a smile that hinted he'd already known I was coming.

A skinny old man with wispy black hair, Marcello was once the pope's private necromancer back in Italy. Story was, he became fixated on rites contained in the more perverse books in the Vatican's infamous library, started freelancing, and earned a visit from the Kindred—a cadre of spooky mystics sort of like the church's version of Navy SEALs.

The runes of exile and censorship branded onto his face and hands looked like burn scars if you didn't know better. They oozed rancid black blood in the presence of magic. The old guy couldn't so much as crack open a fortune cookie or get too close to a church. Or graveyard. Or school.

Dutifully I bowed, pulling from my knapsack a freshly purchased bottle of Olde English 800 wrapped in the requisite brown paper bag. "All hail the king of Canal Street," I said, extending my offering.

"Lovely Leiko, how I missed you. Recent events have left me somewhat morose, pining for better days and the company of dear friends like your father. How is he?"

"Catatonic, last I heard."

"Lucky bastard." Marcello drained his bottle and lobbed it over a shoulder before starting on the one I'd brought.

"Occupational hazard," I said. "Everyone in this racket knows they're one mispronounced incantation or sloppily drawn rune away from bedlam. Or worse."

"Rest assured, luscious Leiko, your father will return. He just went for a little walk between the worlds and got himself lost. It happens to the best of us. But he'll come home again. Sooner or later," Marcello winked, "everyone comes home."

"I've come for something more pressing than a reunion."

"To the point then." Marcello gulped from the bottle and wiped his mouth with the back of one scabby hand. "After all, Marble Lives Matter."

"Somebody in this city disagrees."

"Somebody always does. A side effect of that freedom you Americans are so famously proud of."

"Italy is also a democratic country, Marcello."

"But Vatican City is not. Whatever differences the supreme pontiff and I may have, that strange little nation truly respects its monsters. Luminous Leiko, have you seen Michelangelo's *The Last Judgment*? Zealous martyrs abound in the End Times. Saint Bartholomew proudly holds his own flayed skin. Saint Catherine joyfully poses alongside the wheel on which she was broken. And in the center, a supreme God King presides over beautiful blazing Armageddon. Salvation by force? Now that's monstrous."

"You put a lot of stock in monsters. Tell me, what happens when we run out?"

"There is always the same amount of evil at work in the world." His slitted gaze passed over the surrounding tenements. "If there are no more monsters, people will have to take their place."

As if on cue, sirens wailed, startling a flock of birds into noisily fleeing a nearby rooftop.

"It's happening already," Marcello said. "Can't you see?"

I took from my pack the baggie containing pieces of demolished gargoyles I'd collected. "Whoever is doing this leaves the stone itself structurally altered. The statues cannot be repaired, not even by magic."

Marcello gave the evidence a cursory look, then tossed it back to me. "That would require an alchemist," he said, nipping the bottle.

"There are no more alchemists."

"Are you sure about that?" Marcello tipped his head back for a longer drink.

"You know damn well Chase was the last of his order. That's why my father partnered with him in the first place."

"Yes, the *late* Chase Grayson."

"You, of all people, have doubts?" I could hear the anger in my voice and didn't bother to rein it in. "It was you, your highness, who negotiated the city contract for the ritual that sent Chase and my father into the subway tunnels. Earned yourself a handsome commission, if I'm not mistaken."

Marcello nodded. "One of many thorns in my crown."

"All they found of Chase was an arm, his right one. And it destroyed my father's mind, whatever happened to them down there."

He leaned forward, elbows on his knees, and rolled the paper-wrapped bottle slowly between his palms. "Would you like to know what did happen?"

"I'd ask my father, but he's not reachable just now."

Marcello's knowing grin returned. "Not by you."

That, I hadn't expected. "Aren't you already on thin ice with the Kindred?"

"I believe your culprit has saintly ambitions." Speaking softly, Marcello fixed his bloodshot stare on some obscure distant point. "Everything feels like it's ending. And I am less prepared than most for the final judgment."

There is a special breed of silence on the catatonic ward of a hospital that exists nowhere else. Orderlies called it the Vegetable Patch when they thought doctors and visitors could not hear them, implying some organic process or growth, however undetectable, was at work. But I believed that particular silence existed outside of nature. I imagined it's the way the universe sounded before life began.

I used a spell to get us past the cameras and alarms while remaining unseen by the staff. Despite billing me for the service, the orderlies hadn't shaved my father's face or cut his hair in years. Reclining on the narrow bed, eyes closed and hands folded, with his long white mane and matching beard, he looked like the old karate master in a '70s kung fu flick.

At least the sheets were clean.

The only indications my father was alive in that tiny room were the barely perceptible rise and fall of his chest and the steady beeping of the machines to which he was attached by a forest of tubes and wires.

"Still jealous?" I asked Marcello as he lit three candles made from the fat of an executed killer and poured a circle of salt around the bed.

"Laughable Leiko, you should see some of the places I've slept in."

Black beads were already sprouting on his face and hands and I stood back, trying to ignore the pungent stink. I wasn't sure why Marcello was putting himself in danger on my account, but then I remembered my lack of progress so far. And I remembered Chase too. Would I ever love somebody else like that? *Could I?* The sparkling flash in his cool dark eyes when he smiled had been warmer and brighter to me than summertime sunshine. I recalled how good it felt when our fingers entwined. I saw his severed right arm lying on a slab in the city morgue. And I said nothing as the necromancer began his ritual.

If Marcello was out of practice, it didn't show. The air grew dense, filling with the stench of sulfur as he performed the chants and made the gestures that were the purview of his macabre order.

"A situation like this," Marcello said, tiny rivers of blood trickling from his skin, "we're basically ringing a payphone. I can't promise it'll be your father who answers."

"I know."

And when my father's body sat up, the being whose reptilian eyes looked at us from inside his skull was terribly ancient and utterly inhuman. It used my father's mouth to growl something in Latin, but Marcello shouted back in Italian. A smile crept over my father's face and the entity within him responded in kind. Italian being more Greek to me than actual Greek, I didn't catch but a few words of their exchange: traitor, hopeless, recompense (or maybe it was retribution?).

There was something else too, a word the creature repeated several times that I didn't know.

Marcello seemed to demand some kind of answer or explanation as the machines surrounding my father smoked and sizzled. The overhead lights flickered. Slowly, my father turned toward me, alien eyes gleaming with undisguised interest.

Just as his lips parted to speak again, Marcello broke through the circle of salt and splashed his blood across the hideously smiling face, bellowing an incantation I didn't recognize in a language I'd never heard.

The candles flared, blindingly bright, and the machines all died at once, causing an alarm to sound throughout the hospital. My father's body went limp, his eyes closed, and his chest resumed its normal rhythm—weak, but steady.

"That word it kept saying," I asked. "What does it mean?"

"Slaughter." Marcello wiped fetid blood from his face with the edge of a blanket. "It was just a taunt."

"What else did it tell you?"

"Nothing," he said. "It doesn't matter anyway. Demons lie all the time."

———

I allowed Marcello his secret for the moment. He was clearly shaken by what the fiend said, but refused to tell me anything more. It was personal, he insisted. Something to do with his time at the Vatican.

The next evening, I sat on the patio outside a tavern near the university, attempting to buoy my spirit with spirits, ignoring the worrisome runes in the cloudy ice cubes and debating which gargoyle I might stake out, when a busker approached. She strummed her guitar and leaned close, forcing eye contact. A pale girl with dirty dreads and a cute face filled with almost as many piercings as freckles. I searched my jeans for a dollar, which she made no move to accept.

"Your presence is requested," she said, "for a royal audience of the utmost importance."

"Requested? Or demanded?"

She giggled and plucked a high string, the fading daylight glinting on her metal decorations. "The king of Canal Street begs your indulgence, miss. I'm told the matter is urgent."

I drained my glass and followed the twinkling troubadour, some magic of her own making the trip take only a moment. The city seemed to move around us, blurry and indistinct, as her thin fingers danced across the guitar. She strummed an echoing last note and we stood in the weed-choked lot that was Marcello's throne room.

The king was seated on his bench, as usual.

Except for his head, which was missing.

The girl dropped her guitar and wept as I approached the decapitated corpse. The wound was neat and cauterized, there was no blood aside from the toxic ichor congealing on his hands; further proof of the presence of magic. I barely noticed the girl come to kneel at Marcello's side.

"Who did this?"

"An agent of the church maybe. Or some servant of Hell. Marcello had many enemies, upstairs and down, on both sides of the veil. When did you see him last?"

"Midday. When he sent for you."

Taking the head was a message from Marcello's killer. No resurrection would be possible, not even communion. It seemed his own final judgement had come. But you had to have known the king to spot the other, less obvious message. One that only he could have left.

A tallboy between his legs, not a bottle.

No brown bag in sight.

Not some cheap rotgut malt liquor, but a local craft beer.

The can was still cold when I picked it up to examine the label: Universal Elixir Pale Ale, a product of Left-Hand Path Brewing Company. One severed arm raising a frosty mug.

The girl, seeing my expression, asked, "What's wrong?"

"Everything," I said. "Every single thing."

I adopted a burly masculine glamour to enter the brewery. A cozy room of wood and stone in the basement of a boutique hotel downtown.

Chase was behind the bar, empty right sleeve of his denim shirt pinned up. He looked the same except his hair was shorter now, shot through with premature silver. Clearly, he wasn't trying to hide.

And why hide? Until yesterday, nobody was looking for him.

I arrived late and only a few tables were still occupied. At the bar, I sipped a draft and watched my father's former protege, the first great love of my life, fill glasses and chat with patrons. The look of dull passivity on their faces and gently spreading warmth in my own belly told me there was more than alcohol at work in Chase's brew. I made a point to drink slowly.

Chase barely looked at me until the last stragglers settled up and stumbled outside. He locked the door and put a fresh beer in front of me, without asking, then reached out to kiss the back of my fat hairy hand.

"You look sexy in a beard, Leiko."

I'd had more faith in my own abilities. The flutter in my chest both thrilled and humiliated me. "How did you know?"

"You weren't even old enough for a drink the last time I saw you." Chase's smile did not reach his eyes and there was none of the mischievous flash I'd loved. "But I would know you with any face—anytime, anywhere. I'm surprised, but I wasn't fooled. How'd you find me?"

"An old friend."

"Of course." Chase poured himself a beer, we clinked glasses and drank. "How fares the king of Canal Street?"

"About a head shorter than yesterday."

It took a moment to register on his face. "It wasn't me, if that's what you're thinking."

"Maybe not." I traced a finger over his palm. "But your hand isn't free of blood, is it? And it's rougher than I remember too. You've been working hard."

"Labors of love are no less taxing." He took back his hand and examined it a moment. "The woman was an accident, I honestly didn't see her. And the guard was self-defense. He pulled a gun, I had no choice."

The lights of the otherwise empty room seemed to dim slightly and I realized I'd grown uncomfortably warm. I let the glamour fade and pushed aside my glass. "You could have not begun this craziness in the first place. What are you doing, Chase? Why now after so many years?"

"What I'm doing," he said, "is saving the world. The timing wasn't entirely up to me. I'm not the only player in the game. Certain things had to be put in motion, circumstances arranged. There was a lot to do before this final stage."

Darkness ringed my vision. I was drenched in sweat. Chase's alchemical skills had only increased with time—I hadn't detected a trace of the powerful sleeping draft.

"Son of a bitch," I mumbled, trying to lift my hand but finding it impossibly heavy. *Still the stupid little girl in love,* I thought. Guess sometimes you really can come home again. I slumped off the stool, striking my chin on the bar, and the hex I fired went wild, shattering the mirror behind him instead of Chase's smirking face.

"Can't believe you did this...to me."

"Knock off that whining." Chase stood over me and his eyes flashed in the old familiar way as he smiled again, for real this time. "I could have just as easily poured a love potion and made you adore me forever."

The lights of the world went out. I couldn't feel the floor beneath me anymore. My tongue was thick and uncooperative.

"Could just...told me...truth."

<hr />

Too cold for tears. It was rain on my face. I was outside, the wind a knife of ice across my skin. It required a great effort to open my eyes.

A rooftop. I didn't know where exactly, but I could smell the heady reek of the waterfront and the peppery tang of tear gas.

Beyond, I saw the city, dark and without power, but lit here and there by the flickering glow of scattered fires. Gunshots rang out. People screamed. Sirens blared.

Chase stood at the roof's edge watching the chaos. His hand rested on the winged shoulder of a massive statue: Samael, the destroyer. A scythe in one marble fist.

I tried to rise silently, but every movement was agony. A groan escaped my throat as I struggled onto hands and knees. Chase turned to watch, his face a frightening blank. On his belt I saw a hammer made of snow-white metal and laced through with veins of an eerily luminescent blue element. Clearly, it was the work of a brilliant alchemist.

His own scythe, I supposed. The weapon with which he planned to slay the Angel of Death.

"Your salvation," I croaked, "doesn't sound to be going too well."

"Change is never easy." He moved away from the ledge and I realized the groaning wasn't coming from me, but the roof beneath us. The building was old, dilapidated. *We truly are on shaky ground here*, I thought, cackling.

"What's so funny?"

"My father said you were no good. I thought he was just being an overly protective daddy and hated him for it. But I see now his problem was with you specifically. He didn't trust you anymore by the end, Chase. And he was right."

I was collecting myself as I spoke, playing for time so as to gather my powers. But Chase's potion must've had some magical dampening property, because it was taking too long. Pain raced through my mind like a rat in a maze. He crouched beside me, rain slicking his silver-tinged hair, and cocked his head as if looking at a creature he didn't quite recognize. The roof sagged beneath us.

"Your father was an idiot."

A nearby explosion shook the building. The roof groaned and buckled further. I felt the familiar thrumming in my arms and fingers again. The agony in my head was fading.

"Tell me all about it," I said. "Air your grievances, you petty little bitch."

He reached out, grabbed a fistful of my hair, and jerked my head back. "I've seen the truth curled around this city's heart," Chase said. "We found it together, me and your father, down in the darkness. The Source of All Shadows. It was here before people and buildings and religions. It was here before the sun. Our ancestors tried to keep it out, wanted to force the world to behave a certain way, but their institutions are weak. We deserve better than we got, Leiko. A new era is dawning and it requires different prophets. We were chosen and made the same offer. We simply elected different paths."

"Traitor." I met his stare and whispered, "Coward."

The hand I used to hold released my hair, formed into a fist, and coldcocked me in the face. I tasted blood as my vision filled with stars—comets, planets, entire goddamn solar systems.

Chase was at the gargoyle with his hammer drawn when I managed to sit up again. Blurry as my vision was, I saw him well enough to read the look of fear and horror on his dripping-wet face as he contemplated what he'd done. I'd like to think maybe he was crying.

"You don't really care about saving the world," I said. "You just wanted to feel more important than you are."

A series of loud snaps, like the bones of a giant being torturously broken, made the roof tremble. My powers were back and the familiar electric feel of magic coursed through my blood.

"This city is going to burn beautifully," Chase said, striking Samael with his hammer and splitting off a ragged chunk of the statue amidst a hail of blue sparks.

"We've outgrown saviors!"

Another blow, more sparks, and the angel lost a wing.

"We've evolved beyond traditions!"

Samael's arm with the scythe was cleaved away and fell, bouncing off the ledge and plummeting toward the street far below.

Chase glared at me. "We don't need monsters."

I saw the crack appear in the floor as Chase raised his hammer. I opened my mouth—to say what, I have no idea—then closed it again. Another explosion, even closer this time, shook the building again. Gripped by the maniacal fixation that is the greatest strength and weakness of all true believers, Chase didn't notice.

The middle section of the roof caved in and the heavy stone angel toppled backward onto him as the floor split open. Samael and Chase plunged down into darkness together. He didn't get a chance to scream.

I could have warned Chase maybe, or might have saved him with a paralysis hex or levitation spell, if I'd tried.

But if I'm being honest, replaying the moment in my mind, I didn't even consider it.

I watched with wary optimism as the damage caused by the riots and protests of that night was slowly repaired. The election came, ballots were counted, and nearly all the incumbents kept their seats—for better or worse. Something like peace returned to the city, but I couldn't help seeing in the face of every eager volunteer and smiling civic leader another of the potential players in the game Chase spoke of. And Marcello's warning echoed between my ears like the words of a beloved song.

Zealous martyrs abound in the End Times.

Later, I catalogued the last old gargoyles. They'd been relocated to the university museum to be protected and displayed alongside the proper historical context, which seemed the most fitting tribute. They no longer meant what they used to.

I visit my father, cut his hair and shave his face. Inside his room I've placed protection sigils and photographs of us in happier times. I want him to know, when he finally comes home, that he wasn't forgotten.

Sometimes, when I scroll through a particularly bleak batch of headlines or dare to watch the nightly news, when I walk through the city and see a few too many fearful and unhappy looks on the faces I pass, I sense an ominous presence lurking just out of sight. Something ancient, powerful, and unspeakably patient.

The Source of All Shadows, Chase called his master. The truth curled around the heart of the city is, I think, no longer content to remain in darkness. So I've decided to stay home for a while.

In return for waiving a portion of my fee, the council fast-tracked a new public art initiative. The Marcello Tumminelli Memorial Fund engages young creatives to make pieces that will stand in place of the old statues. I am its executive director, sole member of the acquisitions committee, and I admit to having something of a bias.

To put it bluntly: I want more monsters.

Give me better beasts, I tell applicants. New nightmares. Fresh figures onto which we can attach contemporary fears and all our worst impulses.

I long to stroll beneath avatars of Addiction and Illness. On every street corner, I want people posing for selfies with personifications of Loneliness and Debt. Our parks will be filled with children playing in the shadow of Paranoia.

I want gargoyles, I say. And make them fearsome.

This place needs all the monsters we can get.

Struggle as You Will to Rise

I probably won't be able to do this again for a while.

Things are starting to get hectic at home now, with Julianna being so far along. The kids just went back to school less than a month ago, and Maren's acting out, skipping curfew, running around with a bad crowd. Julianna wants to put her into therapy again, if you can believe that. Michael's all right, but we can already tell his grades are going to be a struggle this year. And on top of everything else, work has been a real bear lately. The firm is understaffed, as usual. But I guess you know how all that goes.

Well, maybe you don't. Not anymore.

To be totally honest, it's getting hard to explain the amount of time I spend with you. Julianna actually got a little angry about it this morning. Probably that's just her own guilt. I think she feels weird seeing you now, being so obviously pregnant, and that's why she won't come. It wasn't too bad before she started showing. Now, she said she feels the nurses judging her. And the other night she had a bad dream about you suddenly waking up when she's here. The very first thing you'd see after all this time is your wife pregnant with another man's baby. She started to cry when she told me. It was...touching.

Now then, let me see. I told everyone we finished *East of Eden* last time, so what's next? Maybe something lighter? Tom Clancy? Agatha Christie? How about good ol' Uncle Stevie? I see a copy of *Cujo* right here on top of the pile. That's perfect. And it reminds me that I have something important I need to tell you before I leave.

Would you be all that surprised, I wonder? I mean, about the baby? How much of our chats are you able to retain anymore? It's been a few years, and the doctors tell us your brain activity has decreased dramatically. Still, Julianna worries about what would happen if you did somehow manage to wake up. That's hope for you right there, in all its torturous and hateful splendor.

The kids, on the other hand, they never talk about you. Julianna hasn't even broached the subject of making them come visit for a long time—which is fine with me, obviously. It's so much more fun when it's just us.

Personally, I don't care what the doctors say. I choose to believe you can hear me. Otherwise, what's the point? None of this is any good without you, you know? Do you have any idea how many dusty vegetables I wasted my time reading to before I found you?

You, with your tragic car accident and gorgeous sad wife and pair of cute troubled kids. You think it was easy, winning them over? You're quite a catch, with your fancy house out in that spoiled suburb and really great job with excellent health insurance. Benefits good enough to keep you alive and right here in this bed for a very, very long time.

Man, I just don't know what I'd do without you.

But I think you ought to know she's talking about pulling the plug again. Julianna said that way she could begin *transitioning to a new life phase* and *commence the grieving process in earnest* — I know, I know. Goddamn shrink must charge by the word, am I right?

But she said if you weren't around then we could get married. She thinks it would be better for the baby that way. I'll tell you, when I think about what my life would be like if I couldn't come here and talk with you anytime I wanted...

But don't worry, I'll change her mind. Don't I always?

God, you should see how beautiful she is right now. It's kind of sexy too, which I didn't expect. Actually, I guess you did see her like that, didn't you? Twice, in fact. But I can't help but wonder if she was so very, well, let's say *affectionate* during the other two. Know what I mean? Because I'll tell you, man, your wife is more down for it than ever these days.

One of my new favorite things to do is skip out of work early and make a move just before Maren and Michael get home from school—being sure to leave the bedroom door open a crack, of course. I personally think it's healthy for kids to understand about sex, don't you? And she makes the cutest noises, doesn't she? When I spread her out and shove my—

—"instincts in this matter are typically right on," said the veterinarian. "There's no reason to think it's anything other than a simple case of—"

Oh, hello, Nurse Peterson. I didn't see you come in. How's it going?

We just started a new one today, actually. I know, right? I totally agree. I'm more into the classics myself, but Julianna told me King was his favorite. To each his own, I always say.

Hey now, is that what I think? Lord, not one of Nurse Klein's infamous brownies! For me? You temptress. Thank you very much. No, I think we're just fine. Thanks again for this. What a treat!

I swear, man, if the smell of this delicious brownie isn't enough to wake you up, I think all hope is truly lost. Damn, that's tasty. Anyway, what was I saying?

Oh, right. My new favorite game. Suffice it to say, sound carries in that big house of yours—and I make sure there's plenty of sound to go around.

The best part is knowing all my fun would be shut down right away if one of your kids just had the guts to say something to Julianna. There's no way she knows they can hear us. And if she did? If she realized they overheard some of the *really* filthy things I make her say? But it doesn't matter because they're gutless. Those pampered little brats of yours are obviously uncomfortable and embarrassed about what's happening, and yet they'd rather sit and fester silently in this delicious little stew of dysfunction I'm cooking up.

Were they always so weak, I wonder? Or did your ending up in this bed do that to them? My own childhood was certainly no picnic and I turned out fine. Ultimately, I think it's a question of genetics.

Regardless, another recent discovery of mine is how much fun it is to shrink Maren's clothes. She's turning into quite a little hottie, your daughter. But you know teenage girls—it's just too easy! Pants get a little snug and right on cue she insists on eating in her room— *while studying,* of course—wearing baggy sweatpants and hoodies all the time. Julianna thinks it's just a phase, but I really believe with a little hard work I can get her cutting by Christmas.

It helps that she's being bullied online pretty seriously. I don't mind telling you it was no small chore to coordinate at first, keeping track of all those different accounts. Reluctant as I was to write anything down, I finally started using a password log and that streamlined the process. People can be so cruel on the Internet.

Boy, I really wish I knew for sure that you can hear me. This was fun for a while, but I have to say it's getting kind of sad. Your pulse doesn't change anymore when I fill you in on the latest news, and when was the last time your eyelids so much as twitched for me? Do you even care about your family? I thought we had something special here.

Anyway, what else? Let me think...

As entertaining as Maren can be, it's Michael who might have some actual potential. He's only fourteen, so it's a tad early to say for sure, but we shared a kind of special moment together the other day, which left me hopeful. I caught him watching—

—"*as the dog sat beneath the shade of a large tree and eyed the car's slow approach, a cloud of dust rising—*"

Can I help you?

No, I'm sorry. I haven't seen the doctor around today. Nurse Peterson was in earlier, but it's just been me and this guy since. That's right, Stephen King. Yeah, he's great, isn't he? One of my favorites. Okay, you do that. Have a good one.

I never liked that orderly. Something about the way he looks at me, it just creeps me out. Hell, he's probably just jealous he isn't the one sleeping with your wife. She's a celebrity of sorts among the staff here—among the men anyway. Don't think for a second that pompous young doctor of yours wasn't trying to get in her pants. Lucky for you, I showed up first.

As I was saying, the boy had Googled himself a bit of, shall we say, *adult* entertainment? And I just happened to walk into his room at a particularly embarrassing moment. But don't you worry, I did the right thing. We had a frank and earnest man-to-man talk about how what he was doing was perfectly natural and nothing to be ashamed of. I even showed him some choice websites that wouldn't infect his computer with any malware or viruses. Websites that specialize in a very *specific* type of content, if you know what I mean.

Having monitored his web activity for a few weeks now, I'm hopeful he and I will turn out to have more in common than I expected. He seems to have a thing for redheads, your son. Especially when they're hogtied and crying.

But before I forget, there is one bit of bad news I have to share.

Try as I might, I never could get Coco to like me. That dog, no matter what I did or how many treats and toys I bought her, we were oil and water, my friend. Or maybe it was more like we were oil and gasoline: keep us near each other and eventually somebody was going to get hurt. Well, it finally happened.

See, I didn't care if she liked me or not. I didn't mind the growling or occasional destroyed shoe. I was willing to let bygones be bygones because I know it was you who bought her for the kids when she was just a puppy. And she was the last thing of yours still in the house, since I convinced Julianna to put every picture of you into storage and out or sight.

Hey, it was that or pull the plug! I told her it would be like practice, that we'd move on together *in incremental emotional stages—* think I got that particular piece of psycho-babble from Oprah. Pretty good, right? Or maybe it was Dr. Phil? Whatever, it worked.

All I'm saying is that I did my best with the dog for your sake. But the other day she bit me and I cannot allow that. Like my father always said, the man of the house must project a certain stature. He must cultivate a level of authority at all times. Every ship needs a captain and the captain calls the shots, and that filthy mutt bit me right on the goddamn leg and Julianna, *she laughed.*

I know, right? But what did you really think was going to happen? The days of a woman standing by her man are long since passed. Just look at the state of the world today and tell me if anybody's in charge anymore. Hell, look around this room right now. Do you see your wife here with you? Where's the support? That's what I'd like to know.

Maybe it's my fault for expecting better from her. I think that girl of ours needs a lesson, my friend. It's been too long and she's forgotten the rules. I've been too lenient.

It's the pregnancy, I think, that got my guard down. But it's okay, I'm not worried. Julianna's due any day now, and the kids are in school again, so it will be just her and the baby at home. Just her and the baby and me.

I've got vacation time saved up, plus some paternity leave coming my way—it's a very progressive company. And she's a clever girl, Julianna. I think it won't take her long, if provided with a little *extra* attention, to understand how things are going to be from now on. For the baby's sake, if nothing else, she'll get with the program.

Well, well, well, what have we here? You haven't had a pulse that high in months.

Yes, hello again, Nurse Peterson. I know—I'm as surprised as you! Blame Stephen King, I guess. It is a pretty scary story, I have to say, and so violent. You have to wonder what kind of person thinks up stuff like this.

No, of course we can't expect any permanent improvement at this point. But there's no harm in hoping, isn't that right? A measurable reaction like this could mean that a little part of him is still in there somewhere, isn't that so? I'm certainly no expert, but I like to think that maybe, in a way, he can still understand what I'm saying.

Yes, I hope so. And thank you for checking on us so quickly.

No, actually I'm afraid I have to be going. Our dog ran away last week and the children have been very upset. If I can, I like to be at the house before they get home from school in the afternoon.

But you will be sure to tell Doctor Patel about this exciting little development, won't you? Between you and me, I think he might be encouraging Julianna to consider making a rather hasty decision, and perhaps this will convince him not to give up. Thanks very much.

It's funny, but I honestly don't know what I'd do without this man. Sometimes it seems like he's my only real... Well, it's a little embarrassing to admit, and it may sound strange. Can I tell you a secret, Nurse Peterson?

I think I enjoy these visits more than he does.

'Till the Road Runs Out

The ratty doublewide burned faster than they expected, and when the whiskey-fueled flames reached the meth lab in the trailer's back bedroom, the explosion was likewise extraordinary.

Hicks gulped the last of the Jack Daniel's, wiped his mouth with his hand. The flames were warm against his shirtless torso, his muscles hard and lean from his most recent turn inside. He leaned back on the Mustang's hood, feeling toasty inside and out, as he was tickled by the heat of the fire and the fuzzy embrace of booze. He ran a hand over his fresh buzz cut, crossed one booted ankle over the other, and casually lobbed the empty bottle into the fire.

He cast an admiring glance at Dakota. He looked hot, like something out of a vintage heavy metal video, standing near the trunk in tight jeans, black boots, and a tank top. Platinum highlights streaked through his long, raven-hued hair. Dakota hugged himself and watched his childhood home burn, a cocky smirk on his glossy lips. Hicks felt something at his feet and looked down to see a fat orange cat rubbing against him. He kicked it, not hard. It hissed. He chuckled.

Dakota stepped over, slapped his shoulder, and picked up the cat. "Asshole," Dakota said, nuzzling it lovingly. "Be nice to my pussy."

Hicks shoved off from the car and pulled Dakota close, the warm cat pressed between them. He grabbed a handful of that luscious dark hair and pulled, just hard enough, the way Dakota liked, and said, "Fuck your pussy."

Dakota's tongue snaked out and licked Hicks' stubbly chin. "Promises, promises."

"First things first," Hicks said. They kissed, the fire roaring before them. "First we see the Duke, sell this shit." He looked at Dakota, looked him up and down real slow, like he enjoyed every inch of the view. "Then we'll take care of the rest."

Hicks opened the passenger door, and Dakota slid in, petting the cat. Hicks slammed it shut and walked around, grabbing his jacket from atop the pile of bags in the back seat through the open window. It wasn't much to look at, but it was everything worth taking from this place—plus a shitload of crystal.

Whatever else he'd been before he became barbecue, Dakota's father had been a hell of a cook. He'd offered up his whole stash before Hicks introduced his face to a shotgun. A right nice gesture. Of course, they were taking the stuff anyway. And his money. And his guns. His blubbery apologies were years too late for Dakota, and Hicks had done worse things for less worthy causes. Killing that S.O.B. had just been the cherry on the sayonara sundae on their way out of this pit.

"That was so hot, babe," Dakota said. "The way you made him cry."

Hicks put on his coat and slipped into the driver's seat, gunned the engine, and spared one more look at the conflagration. "Didn't I tell you I'd take care of it?"

Dakota hugged the cat. "Do you love me?"

"All the way, baby. 'Till the road runs out."

He threw the hotrod into gear, peeled out and made for the highway, bearing down hard, chasing—and finally gaining on—his own little bloody slice of the American dream.

———

The Mustang devoured road. The engine roared like a hungry beast as they sped west into the humid North Florida night. Hicks turned his head and Dakota slipped a Marlboro between his lips, holding out the flaming Zippo. He sucked deep and pressed down on the gas. Ozzy wailed from the radio. Waffles slept on the bags.

"What kind of name is Waffles for a cat?" Hicks asked.

Dakota only shook his head patronizingly, as if the question were too stupid to bother with, and lit a cigarette for himself.

Hicks said, "Good thing you're pretty."

Dakota rolled his sparkly eyes and smiled. He could be on his way to the grocery store instead of fleeing a murder scene. Hicks liked that. He'd been concerned that Dakota was all talk in the joint, and he'd watched real close for signs of doubt back at the trailer. When Dakota kicked things off, breaking a lamp over dear old Dad's head, Hicks had known he was for real, and he'd been glad. He had every intention of making off with the goods either way—alone, if need be. But that's not how he wanted it. Not anymore.

Hicks wasn't nervous either. He felt no guilt. The speeding was more for the joy of the ride, his love of his car and the rush of newly reclaimed freedom, than fear of getting caught. The cops didn't come here unless they had to. No neighbors in the trailer park would have called them because they all had secrets of their own to hide. The fire department would come, but even after they found the body it would look like another meth lab accident. By the time the so-called authorities figured how Brad Chambers actually bought it, they'd be long gone.

Hicks was calm—though he wouldn't be *totally* at ease until after their meeting with the Duke. He didn't like drugs and he hated drug dealers, hated their fake-ass tough guy posturing and drama. Still, there was nobody better to help them unload a stash this size. The money wouldn't be exactly fair, but it'd be pretty close. And for now, pretty close was close enough. He pulled a pistol from between the seats, switched it to his left hand.

"What are you doing?" Dakota asked.

Hicks aimed at the highway marker and pulled the trigger without slowing down. A hole exploded in the green metal sign overhead, a crater replacing the dot above the "i."

"Show-off," Dakota said. His flirty giggle made Hicks think about porch swings and camp fires, sunny beaches and snow on Christmas, cold beer in the morning and hot sex at night. All good things.

Hicks replaced the gun. Dakota leaned over and lay on his chest, one hand moving under his jacket, lazily stroking the smiling devil tattoo on Hicks' stomach. The kid was asleep in seconds. He wasn't really a kid, of course. But he seemed so young to Hicks that sometimes there wasn't anything else to call him. Hicks snuck a peek down, feeling Dakota's warm, rhythmic breathing on his chest, and watched his lover's closed eyes twitch.

He'd been sneaking glances at the kid for days, thinking about not thinking about him, after Dakota first arrived inside, long before they actually met. It was Dakota's first time in a real prison, and it showed. Hicks saw the kid take a few beatings, but hadn't stepped in. He was a career con doing his own time and only wanted to be left alone. Helping people got you killed, he knew that for certain.

Though Hicks had still not been able to help himself from thinking about the new arrival with the pretty eyes.

Theirs was not a meet-cute by any Hollywood standard; not even by porno standards. But we don't get to choose who we love in this world, Hicks thought, no more so than we get to choose how we meet them. He'd come across two big Aryans going at the kid and hadn't thought twice. Having caught them with their pants actually down, he had all the advantage he needed and more.

By the time the guards responded, Hicks had painted that cell in a fresh coat of red blood. To the hole he'd gone, but it was a small price to pay. When he came back to the block, Dakota was waiting for him. They started talking. When Dakota got out, there were letters. Letters became phone calls, visits. By the time Hicks was released, they had a plan. He'd made a few calls, picked up his car, and come calling on Dakota.

Happiness isn't just for pretty people, Hicks thought. It's not just for rich people, smart people, or even just for nice people. After a lifetime of tough breaks and raw deals, bad choices and worse luck, he figured it was only fair that even a broken-down con inching ever further past forty had the right to a shot at some happiness in this fucked-up world. Everyone should get a chance, and this was his. He knew he wouldn't get another.

But that was okay. One was all he needed.

He'd always been a good shot.

—◦◦◦—

A solitary figure was stumbling down the dirt road, and Hicks could smell his happy ending begin to rot.

There shouldn't be anybody out here, he thought. That's the point of the spot. The Duke didn't hold court in Nowhere, Alabama, for the scenery. It was a lonely place a million miles from anywhere a sane person would want to be. He flicked on the high beams, recognized the wounded man, and realized that as bad as he thought it might be, things were actually much worse. He threw the car into park.

"Stay here," Hicks said as he grabbed the pistol and got out. Before him the man fell to his knees into a widening pool of blood, squinting dazedly into the car's lights.

"Georgie?" Hicks said, kneeling to look the man over closely. "It's Hicks. What happened? Where's your brother? Where's Duke?"

Slowly, Georgie turned to look at Hicks and his bruised lips spread into a lazy smile. "I got guts," he said, voice cracking with a sudden, tittering giggle. "I got guts, Hicks. So much guts."

He really did. They were in his hands.

Cupped near his waist, Georgie carried two handfuls of dripping intestines. A few loose ends dangled absently, having slipped through his fingers. Blood and bile oozed out of the ragged gash in his stomach beneath a silk shirt that had once been white. Dakota's door opened, but Hicks waved him back. He grabbed Georgie's shoulder and shook him. "Where's Duke? Who did this to you?"

"*Santa Muerte,*" Georgie whispered.

As cold as it was, Hicks' heart was gripped by icy fingers of fear at the words. *Saint Death.* A folktale god, deity of the damned. The skeletal Madonna was the patron saint of murderers, drug dealers, and even more deranged members of the underworld. Hicks had seen tattoos and prayer cards in the joint. Most of it was harmless, a sort of grass-roots religion among the new outlaw class. Like all religions, though, it had fanatics. And they were maniacs.

This was as ugly as could be. Legit Death Heads were bad news: a cult of criminals who worshipped the Grim Reaper. If Duke and his boys ran afoul of lunatics like that, there would be nothing left of them to save—not that Hicks was interested in coming to their rescue. What he wanted was much more practical than salvation.

"Georgie," Hicks said. "Did Duke bring the money?"

No answer. The gutted man swayed on his knees, stared into the headlights.

Hicks tried again. "Did Duke bring the money? Is it still at the spot?"

Georgie retched, the bloody vomit spilling over the mound of exposed guts he cradled.

Hicks grabbed the man's slim ponytail, jerked his head back, and pressed the pistol to Georgie's crotch. He spoke very slowly. "Is my money still at the spot? Answer me, or I swear I'll bury your balls with whatever's left of your brother."

Georgie nodded. "He brings it."

"Tell me where."

———

"You're not serious," Dakota said. "We can't."

"*We* can't." Hicks pushed the Mustang off the dirt road. "I can."

"Bullshit."

"We can't make a new life with a fucking fortune of ice. We need the money."

"I'm going too." Dakota reached into the back seat and grabbed the shotgun.

"No," Hicks said. "I'm just going to have a look around first."

"Then there's no reason I can't go."

Georgie moaned from the passenger seat.

Hicks said, "Don't you bleed in my car, you stupid spic."

Dakota held the gun by the slide and cocked it with one hand. He reached for the blue duffel bag that held the others and slung it over his shoulder, then smiled and blew Hicks a kiss.

"Sissy."

"Bitch." The night wind swept through the sparse trees and silence held sway over the world. One shot, Hicks thought. Make it count. "Fine," he said. "Let's go."

Waffles meowed in the back seat as he watched them leave, and Hicks couldn't help but wonder if the fat bastard was shouting encouragement or a warning at their backs.

The bonfire in the center of the circled vehicles burned brightly, fueled by the bodies of the slain cartel members and the wood and shrubbery gathered beneath them. Duke and his gang were crucified, hoisted up on makeshift timber crosses, blazing before the writhing orgy of carnage below. A pyromaniac's version of Jesus.

Hicks smelled the charred flesh before he saw it. He'd expected the worst and was not disappointed. At his side, he heard Dakota gag.

On the ground, the Death Heads painted each other with the innards of another body. They were naked, emaciated, and awful to see. He'd heard that true believers often starved themselves to look more like their gruesome god. Their skeletal fingers tore slippery pieces from the gaping wound in the dead man's belly, smearing themselves with gore. The body had no head. Hicks saw three of the psychos off to the left, kicking something around like a soccer ball—something with long dark hair.

A putrid corpse dressed in white robes sat before the fire and the burning bodies in a ragged armchair. Dead flowers, along with severed body parts, were scattered around it. Burning red candles encircled the cult's dreadful idol as it watched over the ritual.

Hicks and Dakota sank to the ground outside the light of the fire. Hicks counted at least eight of the cultists, maybe more, in the clearing. Even if there were nine or ten enemies, he might not have hesitated to take them on alone, armed as he was—he'd beaten worse odds. But Death Heads were something else. He eyed a black Durango with tinted windows on the far side of the fire. "There it is. That's where Georgie said it'd be."

Dakota shook his head. "No way."

Hicks said, "I'm getting what we came here for."

"We don't need it. We've got cash already."

"Not enough."

A wail rose up from the gathering by the fire as the Death Heads finally clawed the eviscerated corpse apart.

"Fuck it," Dakota said. "We'll figure something out. Let's just dump the drugs and bail."

The kid didn't get it. He couldn't possibly understand what it had taken Hicks a lifetime of eating shit to learn. Starting fresh, hitting the road with nothing, that's only exciting when you're young. But after starting from scratch again and again, after having nothing for so long, Hicks knew it wouldn't work. Not in the long run, and this time was for keeps. 'Till the road runs out, right? This was his shot. He was going to do it right, and that included getting their money.

They've said that hope is free, that it doesn't cost anything to have faith. *Bullshit.* Hicks knew they were full of it, whoever *they* were, and that hope was plenty expensive. A clean start, safe home, all the operations—the life that Dakota wanted, that he deserved? Hicks tallied these mounting aspirations in his mind's ledger. A better tomorrow cost money. There was a whole lot of hope in the gutter. Hicks had spent enough time there to know.

"Go back and start the car," he said. "Be ready."

Hicks grabbed the bag, got up, and moved into the darkness before Dakota could say anything else. He knew that if he gave himself half a chance, he'd stay. He'd give in and they'd leave with nothing. He walked fast, making his way around the edge of the firelight and staying behind the cars when he could. Dakota's scared, pretty eyes burned in his mind, and the shrieks of maniacs rang in his ears.

Just one more bad thing, Hicks told himself. *Just be that guy one more time and you'll have the rest of your life—your real life, it starts today—to get over it.*

Better men have done worse things.

Hicks reached the Durango and opened the door without being seen. He found the bulky suitcase in the back seat, just like Georgie said. He opened it and began stacking packs of bills into the duffel bag beside the guns. Every squeal and scream from the fire made him jump. When he was finally done, he started back.

About fifteen feet from the SUV, something struck the ground to his left. *The head.* A wild kick sent the dusty severed head flying high, arcing through the air to land, bounce, and roll to a stop right next to him. The cult was quiet as all of their hollow eyes turned and stared at him in unison. Hicks leveled the shotgun.

The Death Heads fanned out and began to approach. Hicks thought of ordering them back and dismissed it. Even if they understood, they would not care about his threats. They loved death. What other threat could he offer? He tucked the shotgun under his arm and drew two pistols from his jacket pockets. The Death Heads were closing in fast, clawing their own flesh with sharp, dirty fingernails, working themselves up into a frenzy of bloodlust.

Hicks opened fire.

The tall bald man on his far left took the first shot in the chest and went down quickly. On his right, Hicks managed to hit a woman in the shoulder. She spun around and fell, but kept crawling toward him. His second shot found her head.

Hicks kept shooting as he backed toward the Durango. The seven left were spread farther out now, flanking him in the dark like Halloween decorations come to life. He kept shooting at the four he could see.

Reaching the car, Hicks dropped the bag and shotgun by his feet. He rested against the vehicle and sighted a man with a grizzly beard. The first shot hit his chest, the second, his neck. Hicks moved on instantly to a young girl nearing him on the right. She was close. He could smell her. The reek of shit, blood, and vomit made his eyes water.

He pulled the trigger, and the gun clicked empty. He tossed it, tried the other one. Same story. He reached down and came up with the shotgun just as she lunged, emptying both barrels into her stomach and cutting her in half in mid-air. Splattered with a warm rain of blood and guts, Hicks dropped the empty shotgun and pulled another pistol from the bag. The only sound as he scanned the dark was the crackling of the fire.

Pain erupted in his shoulder and Hicks screamed.

From the roof of the Durango, a young boy wearing a necklace of bones raised a long wooden spear and plunged it down again. Hicks tried to duck, but the spear sank into his back. He stepped away and shot the boy, saw him fall silently from the roof.

Suddenly, he was knocked to the ground. The spear fell from his back, and the wind rushed from his lungs. A big man loomed over him, brandishing a machete. Hicks raised the pistol, but the lunatic brought the large blade down onto the back of his hand. Several of his fingers fell cleanly away, and Hicks saw himself drop the gun.

With a shrill cry mismatched to his size, the man raised the blade high above his head. Hicks, half-blind with pain and struggling to breathe, kicked as hard as he could up toward the man's dangling genitals. The big man doubled over, clutching himself, as Hicks rolled out of reach.

Getting shakily to his feet, Hicks saw the other three coming closer: two women and a man with his long hair slicked back and shiny with fresh blood. Hicks reached into his boot and pulled out his hunting knife, tucking his wounded hand close to his chest.

A sound erupted from the far side of the fire, one Hicks knew well. Two bright spotlights grew large in the dark as Hicks' car burst over the hillside, flying through the air like a V8-powered magic carpet. The Mustang came down hard and clipped the seated corpse idol. It sailed into the fire, chair and all, as the car skidded to a stop, flinging dust and gravel.

Hicks smiled as he saw Dakota at the wheel, looking mad as hell. He leapt out, blasting away with a sawed-off pump-action like he'd been born to do it. The girls scattered, and the long-haired man scurried behind a nearby pickup.

The big man with the machete, though, having recovered from the shot he'd taken to the balls, ran straight at Hicks.

Dakota, too far away to shoot without hitting Hicks, watched him and the man with the machete meet in a bone-snapping collision. The big man landed on top of Hicks, who thrust his blade desperately up, gouging into the lunatic's left eye. Distantly, he felt the rusty blade of the machete push deep into his stomach. An enormous pressure crushed his neck.

His vision failing, Hicks tore his knife free from the big man's eye socket and stabbed it into the side of his neck, pulling down as hard as he could. The Death Head's throat ripped apart like a soggy garbage bag, spilling blood and stringy bits of muscle and flesh onto Hicks' face. Still, the maniac squeezed his neck and pushed the machete up deeper into Hicks' belly. It felt like the tip was in his chest, poking a lung. Every breath was agony. The handle jutted out from the mouth of his laughing devil tattoo like a strange black tongue.

Dakota appeared above them suddenly and emptied a small pistol into the big man's back. The maniac finally slumped over and was still, and Hicks fell into blackness.

The screech of jamming gears roused Hicks. He forced his eyes open and saw the world rushing past outside the car. His hands were heavy in his lap, one wrapped in a stained sweatshirt and throbbing. A sticky, warm puddle squished beneath his ass as he tried to sit up. Pain—indescribable pain—pushed him back down.

"Hold on," Dakota yelled, tears streaming from his eyes. His foot slammed the gas pedal to the floor. "Hold on, Hicks."

Hicks tried to speak, but found his tongue was too heavy. He blinked hard and saw the blue bag at his feet—feet he could not move—spilling over with cash. The kid would be okay. He could be anything he wanted, whoever he wanted to be. In countless mirror and window reflections over the years to come, that sly, sexy, beautiful smile could be Hicks' memorial. On whatever face the kid chose, beneath any hair, that smile would sit resolutely below those wonderful, sparkly eyes, just for him. Not a bad legacy, Hicks thought. Better men have checked out with less.

And where was Georgie? Only Waffles stared back at him from the back seat, ambivalent, as if he were not surprised by these recent grim developments. Hicks decided that he didn't care. It was getting hard to focus. He threw up, and spit and blood spilled down over his chest. It pooled in his lap on the already sodden blanket that was wrapped tightly around him like a big plaid bandage.

"You just hold on," Dakota said. "Just hold on! All the way, remember? 'Till the road runs out."

But the road was ending. Dakota couldn't see it yet, but Hicks could. A large black tunnel was approaching just up ahead, swallowing the horizon. They were speeding right toward it. Hicks saw the sun rising behind them in the side mirror. They were driving west. If you drive west fast enough at dawn, Hicks thought, it's like you're driving into the past, back into yesterday.

Hicks didn't care much for yesterday, not any of the yesterdays he'd known. He wished he could have been born later. Maybe the world of tomorrow would have been his time. He'd been too early, and now it was way too late. But maybe that's what it would take. Maybe he was the kind of guy that fueled the machines of progress. The pain flowed out of him then, sudden as a blink, and with it the regret. It was silly to regret. He'd had his shot, after all.

The world doesn't care if you're in love. It doesn't care about your regrets or your promises. It doesn't owe you anything. The world is full of monsters. They grow out of slinking under beds and crouching in closets, and they get worse. Once, a little boy named Garrett Hicks thought you could beat those monsters if you were tough, if you made yourself scary enough. So he'd bloodied his knuckles, sharpened his tongue, cultivated a good glare and big, hate-filled muscles. He injected an armor of ink beneath his scar-covered flesh to hide the cracks.

It worked for a while. But he learned too late that grown-up monsters don't fight like that. They're carved of brick and steel, made of disappointment and regret, and they're relentless. In order to take down those monsters, you have to have the right ammo and you've got to be very quick. There are no second chances, none that ever really count. It's not fair, but in the world of grown-up monsters, hate is a half measure and even love is most often a bullet of insufficient caliber. Maybe tomorrow it would be enough. Hicks had time to hope—quickly, just before the darkness got too deep—that it would.

Dakota was shouting. It sounded faint and very far away. They drove into the tunnel, and there was nothing but cool darkness and the lulling pulse of the engine.

Flickering Dusk of the Video God

A fresh burst of white noise roars through my head and jittery tracking lines wiggle and squirm through my vision again, even worse this time. The world stretches and distorts like in a mirror in a funhouse that's no fun at all.

The girl behind the bar pushes my pizza and a sixer of sweaty beers forward, a look of disgust on her small-town pretty face. If this were a movie, she'd be played by Lori Petty, circa a few very hard years after *Free Willy*. She was nicer to me yesterday, even nicer when I first came in four days ago. I know how I look, enacting this, our daily routine, in the same wrinkled clothes again. I know what she's thinking.

I desperately shove my fingers into my eyes until pain stars flare up and drive away the other stuff, blinking hard. Things are normal again, and I realize I know this girl. I've seen her before, and not just in the bar.

She's on the tapes.

For a second, even though it's stupid and doesn't matter, I want to defend myself. It's a reflex. I want to tell the pizza princess that I'm not nuts, that she's not so hot. A Rust Belt eight's an L.A. two at best, baby. Back home, I've kicked hotter than you out of bed for snoring, for hogging the blankets. Ask my ex-wife. I'm still someone who matters. But I've been away from the house too long already.

Money down, sustenance acquired, I go back outside into the dishwater-gray afternoon, into my dad's rattly Buick, and down the only real road in this dead-end Western Pennsylvania town I thought I'd escaped half a lifetime ago.

The world warps again. It's happening more often. The ragged staticky lines do their awful dance and I pull over at the gas station, jamming my fingers back into my eyes until I begin to cry.

A knock on the window makes me jump. Fred—hardware store swami, bestower of king-size Crunch bars at Halloween—leans over me with an enormous CinemaScope smile. If this were a movie, Fred would be played by Brian Cox circa *Super Troopers*. He smiles and raps again on the window, insistent. I roll it down a crack, but just a crack. He's on the tapes too.

"You all right, Davie?"

I nod, wiping away tears with my sleeve.

"Sure is a shame about your old man. We're all real sorry."

His face is doing a strange twitchy thing, movements all herky-jerky like a movie watched in fast forward. His eyes don't match up with his smile, words don't match his lips. The soundtrack for this scene is out of sync.

"Need any help up at the house?" he asks, words coming a full second after his lips cease to move. "Going through their things can be real hard. And your old man, well, he never did throw nothing away, did he?"

I put the car in drive.

"Did he, Davie?" Fred's smile is gone, his face too close to the window "Did he keep...*everything*?"

I start to laugh as I drive away, leaving Fred behind. He looked so painfully earnest, so awesomely dramatic. If this were a movie—not one of mine, of course, but a good one—such a display would never fly, it's too operatic. But in real life, people in crisis often behave like bad actors. Life imitates camp, so maybe my stuff's more realistic than the critics say. I mean, just look at me. Behaving like one of the characters in my own trashy films instead of doing what I know I should and getting the hell out of here.

Past the old white church, abandoned and covered in peeling paint. Stained-glass windows shattered by vandals. Other than that, though, things look shockingly great around here. Aren't places supposed to be worse in reality than memory? Isn't it the real world that comes up short, not time-tinted recollection?

I drive past the grocery store, marquee promising a sale on organic juice. Gone are the discount notices for Mountain Dew by the case. The parking lot is free of young mothers with too many screaming babies clinging to them. I don't see a single obese form straddling a scooter puffing Pall Malls. Gone are the slouching junkie kids and the shambling homeless drones with filth clouds in tow. The sidewalks are even and unbroken. Lawns are clear and mowed. Houses are freshly painted. Good God, is that a jogger?

It's as if a Mayberry filter's been applied to footage of my hometown and that's what I'm seeing projected on the car's windows instead of actual passing scenery. What happened here? I drive past Dad's shop and the familiar neon Video Realm sign, darkened now for good. No point going back there again. All those tapes are just movies.

Four days ago, it was the first place I went. Took a cab from the airport, a two-hour drive and a hefty fare, to find the door wide open, locks busted, tapes scattered all over, and the sheriff (a pudgier young William Hurt, if this was a movie) already there, too eager to help me straighten up and figure out what had been stolen.

"Kids," he said, greedy eyes scanning the scene, looking everywhere but at me.

"Meth heads?"

"Oh no." His face was full of condescending civic pride. "We got none of that around here, thankfully. Not anymore."

Maybe he was right. Nothing was missing. In fact, only the VHS section had been touched at all. The few DVDs and Blu-rays the old man had tentatively begun to stock, the only stuff in the place worth any money, were arranged just as they should be. Nobody cracked the register. Hell, there wasn't even any candy taken. What kind of thieves break into a dead man's movie rental shop to riffle VHS tapes and don't even take any?

I came back and went through the entire inventory the next day. Every copy of every title was accounted for. Of course, by then I'd already found the tapes they'd been looking for. They were at Dad's place the whole time. Safer there, he must have thought. And he was right.

I began to see what happened. Even a Z-grade schlockmeister like myself, the infamous David "Hacksaw" Holland, can put a plot that obvious together. There was no way they could have known I was in New York for a convention. No way they could have known I'd be home in hours instead of days. I surprised them, and nobody had time to check Dad's house before I got there. Now I have the tapes, and they know it too. But what does it all mean? What's happening and who is involved? I'm only halfway through the tapes and already—

Tires squeal as I slam the brakes, jerk the wheel. A huge stag stands in front of the car. Dark charcoal, with an enormous ornate antler spread, eyes shiny and black. It appeared in front of me as if inserted somehow, out of nowhere. I watch it begin to walk away, moving too slowly and then too quickly, like the fast-forward thing is happening again. Like frames of this movie are missing.

The buck looks back once as it bounds away and out of focus. Not out of sight. Not into the woods that line the state road. It just gets blurrier and blurrier until it's gone, worn-out film that's been rewound too many times at last dissolving to nothing.

———

When I get back, the door is open. Someone has been inside, but it doesn't matter because the tapes and ledger were in the trunk of the car. I bring them in, along with the pizza and beer, and get back to it, my own little private film festival.

My father still lived in the same small shabby two-story structure I grew up in, a glorified cottage crouching at the end of a short gravel drive, nearly impossible to see from the paved road if you don't know what to look for. I'm bivouacked in the den, semi-unpacked duffel bag in the corner spilling clothes. I rearrange the VHS tapes in their clear cases into small stacks before the enormous widescreen television—the nicest thing he ever owned—like a miniature plastic Stonehenge.

Bottles of scotch stand ineffective guard around the room, the only thing the old man loved more than movies. He had good taste in both. Authentic classic posters adorn the otherwise drab walls. He was a cineaste of the highest order, my dad, which only made my discovery of the prominent David Holland display at the shop all the more shocking. Two or three copies of all my films—including *To Serve the Devil's Favor*, a hard one to watch even for me—sitting by the register. Each one had a detailed synopsis attached, written in a tight professional script I know well. I didn't think he'd even seen any of my movies, let alone that he'd promote them.

I'm only more certain he didn't kill himself.

The store was somehow thriving. Even in the age of Redbox and streaming services, Frank Holland was the movie man in Pritchard County. In this part of the country, yesterday is sacrosanct and tomorrow is suspect. Being the patrons of quite possibly the last video store in America would have been seen as something to be proud of, another fine tradition being upheld. And poor people are weirdly obsessed with customer service too. Rich folks enjoy automation; they don't want to hear the lawn boy at work. But these people, my people, they know they'll only ever be the boss while exchanging cash for the fleeting, momentary privilege. They liked knowing somebody was there at the video store waiting to serve them.

Also, half the kids who grew up around here worked in the shop at one time or another. I spent most of my young life there. It worked out for all involved: Dad got cheap help; the kids got free rentals; and everybody in town either worked, had worked, knew or were related to somebody who worked there. Hence, the video store was an institution. Hell, more than an hour's drive to the nearest theater, it was practically Hollywood.

It doesn't make sense. Mom died more than a decade ago. He was as over that as he'd ever be. I suppose I can't be certain he wasn't sick himself. When was the last time we even spoke? I can't remember. I ignored so many calls, deleted how many voicemails unplayed? I left him here, all alone. Would I have even believed him, would I have believed any of this, if I had bothered to answer?

He hated guns anyway, never owned one in his life. So I find it hard to believe my old man would have chosen to go out chomping on a pistol, like the sheriff said, even if I could picture him punching his own ticket—which I can't.

I eat little, drink more—two, three beers rapidly. Plastered is my preferred state of mind to work in (nobody sober could have made *Nasty Nuns Tame Sasquatch*) but these are strange waters in which I can take no chances. I stop at three for now, select the next unwatched tape from the nearest wobbly stack, push it hesitantly into the bulky VCR.

The cool feel of plastic, the smooth electronic sound of the tape being accepted, the closing of the little front door, the whirring as it begins to play: familiar and reassuring things I did not realize I missed. I am comforted. The glaring TV screen is the only light in the house and I huddle before it like a campfire, a man lost in the woods, clutching my father's ledger.

Then, the images begin.

I'd thought myself desensitized to violence. Hadn't all the panic-ridden shrinks and parental groups promised that would eventually happen if only we watched enough? I'm a professional provocateur, a connoisseur of atrocities. But this is different. This is real.

In a large empty barn, three men are wrestling with a struggling young girl. She's wearing an oversized t-shirt, hair wild from fitful sleep, eyes wide with panic. Her bare feet and legs are kicking, fighting desperately. If this were a movie—a real movie, I mean—the girl would be played by some unknown. Somebody cheap with great legs.

Over the girl's mouth, muffling her screams, is a thick patch of duct tape. One of the men grappling with her is Fred; good old smiley Fred.

The men never speak. It's clear they don't know about the camera, never once even look in its direction. They tie the girl to a large wooden post and leave. She sobs into the gag. The picture is black and white and grainy, clearly recorded on video with a cheap camera. The sound is scratchy and clipped. A lantern is hung near the girl, cutting out a section from the surrounding dark like a theater spotlight. The contrast of the picture is high, making the edges of the room impossibly black.

My father began to rent video recording equipment along with VCRs at the shop years ago, back when I was still around. It never caught on, but became something of a hobby for him. All movie buffs are frustrated, would-be filmmakers. Our home movies had title cards. Clearly, Dad found a new project to dedicate his talents to late in life.

I do not see the thing in the corner until it moves.

After, I don't know how I missed it. Rewinding the tape, I cannot determine the exact moment it appeared. Maybe it was always there.

Long, thin fingers reach out slowly from the dark. The girl sees what is coming and becomes hysterical. Slowly, the thing comes into the light, flesh the color of neutral gray on a photographic color card. Two long gangly arms, and legs ending in strange clawed feet, snake out from its grossly swollen torso. A pendulous belly droops over its lap, obscuring the thing's gender. I cannot look at it for long. It shimmers and blurs as if it's moving too fast for the tape to capture, even while seeming to be reaching out in slow motion. Tracking lines pull its shape this way and that. My head hurts.

Before, in the other tapes, I'd only glimpsed it. A hand reaching, a blur in the corner, an out-of-focus gray something standing near a ritual, observing a sacrifice, lording over a frenzied orgy and watching the bodies mingle, stroke, fondle, squeeze—always on the edges though. Like a director. Like me.

Now, I see it all.

These people, I realize, the people on the tapes, the people of my hometown, they're performing for this thing. They aim to please it, to entertain it. They serve it. And now I understand, numbly watching as it embraces the squirming girl and begins to sloppily devour her, they also feed it.

Her blood on the hay-strewn floor is too dark, too thick. Romero's chocolate-syrup ichor straight out of '68. It doesn't look real. For a moment the gag comes free and the girl's screams fill the room. I stare saucer-eyed at the glowing screen, crouching still in the dark, ledger forgotten. Quickly, the shrieks die in a wet gurgle.

Christ, Dad, what did you find here?

The gore-streaked thing shuffles silently back into the dark in that same eerie, sputtering way it moved before. Soon, the men return and begin to clean up the scene of the sacrifice. The sheriff is among them this time, along with Fred and several others I recognize. The men of town going about a hard, unpleasant task with the usual stoic determination of rural workers the world over. Blood's just business here. Not unlike any other harvest season, judging by their faces. Some are even smiling.

I review Dad's annotations. He recorded dates, times, and the places where he filmed these things. Camera settings, tape brands. Dozens of locations. He'd been at it for months.

Fast-forwarding to the end proves there is little more to see. The men finish and leave in a speedy rush, and the light of dawn floods in through the open door to fill the empty barn. Finally, the camera is moved, taken from its hiding spot. I see a brief flash of my father's tired old face before he turns it off.

Dad and I talked about movies the way other fathers and sons talk baseball or cars. After Mom died, it was all we had. My memories of my father are all in Technicolor, the good times echo through my brain in Skywalker Sound. His ghost smells like popcorn.

If my life was a movie, he'd be played by Martin Landau or somebody else really good. He deserves somebody good, somebody who'd never be in one of my movies. I know the power of pictures and so did my old man. This documentary project would have seemed to him the best way to combat something he did not understand. It's what I would have done.

I eject the tape and stand in the cold light of the blank blue screen, sipping his scotch from the bottle. I scan the walls of my father's favorite room: *Gentlemen Prefer Blondes* and Gene Kelly's *Singing in the Rain*. Orson Welles stares down at me from a vintage *Citizen Kane* poster. The curdled prodigy's final bitter performance was voicing the planet-eating baddie in *The Transformers: The Movie*. I think of my film school degree, ambitious dreams buried somewhere in L.A. beneath a mound of scripts with titles like *Lesbian Vampire Tramps* and *Revenge of the Jurassic Octo-Sharks* and recipes for fake blood and vomit. I also know something about wasted potential. Guess nobody ends up where they think they will. Ask my second ex-wife.

Outside, a car is trundling down the driveway. Through the window shade I see headlights growing in the darkness. If this were a movie, I'd know what to do. God, I wish this were a movie. I also wish my father had felt differently about guns. But the biggest knife in the kitchen will have to suffice.

I stash the tapes hurriedly in my duffel bag, toss some clothes over them, and move to the door, bottle of whiskey in one hand, enormous knife in the other. I flick on the light above the small front porch, prepared to greet my most unwelcome guest.

It's the pizza princess. Climbing out of a Ford Taurus more rust than red, carrying a fresh six pack and a pizza box. She looks better than she did earlier. A fitted black t-shirt hugs her best assets and her jeans are tight enough to make me concerned about her circulation. She is smiling until she sees the knife. Then she starts to laugh.

"It's a peace pizza," she says. "I promise."

"I already ate. You know I did."

"For tomorrow then. Thought maybe I'd save you a trip."

"Who says I'll still be here tomorrow?"

She walks closer slowly, stepping more into the light. I remember the gray thing on the tape, the way it snuck out into the lantern glare, bit by bit then all at once.

"Stay right there."

"You can relax." She stops walking. "I'm just here to talk. They thought you might listen to me."

"Why?"

She looks sad for a second, then pushes it away. "I didn't think you recognized me. We went to high school together. My name's Heather. You remember?"

I shake my head, eyes on the dark behind her. The sound of crackling static is in my ears again, nagging and distracting.

"I'm not surprised. Three years of meth is like ten years of regular life. Sometimes I don't recognize me either."

"Funny, the sheriff was just telling me how clean this town is."

"He's not wrong, not now. Used to be real bad though."

"Guess the quality of life around here depends on which side of the camera you're on."

"We just want the tapes, Davie. We want the tapes and we want you to go home. You don't belong here anymore. No hard feelings."

There doesn't seem to be anyone else in the dark, but I'm starting to feel foolish posing under the spotlight. A classic Hollywood victim. "Come inside. Slowly."

She follows me in, putting her offerings on the coffee table next to a bunch of empty bottles. "Nobody wants to hurt you."

"Is that what you told my dad? Was it you who blew his head off?"

She looks around the room with a hint of wonder, like someone walking through Graceland or the White House, like she's amazed to be there at last. "That was unfortunate, but it was required. Your father was going to close the shop and take the movies away. He didn't understand."

"That's why you killed him? So he wouldn't close that stupid shop?"

She looks at me, eyes flickering as if lit from within by phantom film projectors. Or maybe it's my eyes that are flickering. Either way, the static is getting louder.

"Your father was killed because the God of the Screen wished it so."

"I've seen the tapes."

"All gods demand sacrifices, Davie."

"You think that thing is God?"

"He's *a* god." She shrugs. "The one that's here. He's the one that cares anyway."

She begins walking around the room, running her hands over the furniture and the posters as if they were sacred relics in an Old World cathedral. I suddenly feel far too sober for this conversation.

"The House of the Purveyor," she says reverently. "It was in your father's films that the God of the Screen appeared to us. Flickers at first, like glitches. We did not yet know how to look. Later, as we learned, He became clearer, His wishes more obvious. But only through your father's films could we see Him, never in any others. We tried. We tried to find Him elsewhere, but we could not. Then, when your father learned what redemption required and could not understand, when he threatened to take the movies away, we did what we had to. We must visit the Realm and conduct the renting ritual. It pleases Him."

She pauses before the television, head bowed slightly. Bathed in the cool blue light, she looks dead. "He saved my life, Davie. I was lost and He found me. I had nothing and He gave me purpose. He saved me, saved the whole town."

I adjust my grip on the knife's handle. "Did he save that girl in the barn? Or how about the kids, the ones on the missing posters my father collected? What did he do for them?"

She smiles, a quick flash of teeth. "He made use of them. It was more than they'd ever do for themselves."

"Time for you to go, Heather."

"Just give me the tapes, Davie. Give them to me and leave. You did it before. You, like so many others, abandoned your home as quickly as you could. All we ask is that you do it again. Go back to California. Go make more movies. We still walk the old roads here, still worship the old gods."

"You rent videos," I say, sneaking a quick gulp of booze. "Not exactly forgotten lore, is it?"

"Nobody reads anymore." She gestures to the tapes, the movie posters. "This is the new ancient. We must have the tapes. Then we will plant them in whatever rental shops remain, and in rummage sales and secondhand stores, and spread His gospel. We will make the world over again, Davie, so much better this time. We'll get it right."

I think of the car accident that killed my mother. Not a drunk. Not an epic pileup. Just a wayward deer, a buck on the road—dark charcoal, eyes shiny and black. Just a plain old everyday life-changing, life-ending accident. It would make a lousy movie.

I think of my father sitting alone in this room with his movies and his booze and a son who ran half a world away to make great art. A son who failed, who didn't answer the phone when it mattered.

I think of *Hacksaw*. Gritty, authentic: the one time I got it all perfect. Someone's remaking it, I hear. Updating my best work already.

Heather turns, begins peeling off her shirt.

"What are you doing?"

"I am for you," she says, undoing her belt. "Tonight, you can do what you like. I am His messenger meant to please you. To show that He wishes you no harm. Tomorrow, you will give me the tapes and go away. We won't hurt you, Davie. You make movies."

She's suddenly naked. There's a black garter tattooed on her left thigh, something a wannabe bad kid would have done. The kind who couldn't afford to run away to California, who didn't have a proud papa waving bon voyage with one hand and dishing out tuition checks with the other, so thrilled over his aspiring auteur, his little future Fellini. It made me sadder than I thought possible.

"But I make *lousy* movies."

"Oh, no." Her eyes are big as IMAX screens and filled with that hypnotic flickering again. "He loves all movies—even yours! Especially yours, in fact. He has often come to us in your work. He favors you, David, Son of the Purveyor. He's in you already."

She's nearly pressed against me. Maybe it's the booze, or the strange pulsing lights in her eyes, or the increasing noises in my head—sounding more like voices all the time—but she is undeniably appealing. If this were a movie, you might be screaming at the screen right now, telling me to get out of there. My father always hated people who did that. So do I.

She reaches out to stroke my face, whispering. Her words are like the rumbling of surround-sound thunder. I feel them in my bones and want to believe the things she says. The television screen begins to strobe behind her. I watch it ignite and die again and again. She leans in to kiss me, so obviously a trap.

If this were a movie, I might even fall for it.

I bring the bottle down over her head. It shatters, covering her hair and face with smoky liquor and bits of glass. But it wasn't how the movies promised it would be. The sound, the feeling, her reaction—it was all so disappointingly real.

Then, suddenly, it isn't.

She looks up, wide eyes full of static. Her gashed face drips scotch, but no blood. She opens her mouth to scream, but only white noise explodes out. She's a dead channel turned to max volume. She grabs for my neck with both hands and I shove the knife forward into the taut muscles of her stomach. Her skin stretches and splits apart like cheap cellophane. The knife, then my fist, is swallowed. Her insides are dry and smooth and cold.

I shove, and she falls limply to the ground like a zombie shot through the head. The knife is tangled in the long black tendrils of her film-strip guts, plastic entrails that shine in the quickly strobing light. They stretch out from the void in her stomach like the tentacles of a parasite Cronenberg would dream up, unspooling farther as she crawls away to lean against the wall.

She looks from the hole I gouged into her, up from her own dangling celluloid parts, to me, test pattern eyes brimming with tears. "I was all used up, Davie. I was dead and He began my life again. He *rewound* me."

I pull the knife free of the shimmering strips, move quickly to stand over her. Raising it high, knowing already what I'm going to do.

"I hate remakes."

The blade went in easily through her eye, nearly up to the hilt. Light spills from the gash, filling the room. I stab her again and again until that light goes out at last, until she lies down and is good and still and stays that way.

There's no blood. The television goes dead. Fade to black. Roll credits. That's a wrap, people.

Except it's not.

In my business we call this part the Third Act.

The finale.

If this was a movie, there'd be very serious music playing over a quick series of cuts showing yours truly hurriedly getting things together. An awesome '80s-style montage of packing up the car. I've got the bag full of Dad's tapes, three bottles of that fine scotch, and a tank half-full of gas. The cigarette lighter in Dad's junky old Buick still works fine, one of the only parts that does. And I've got a neon-crowned chapel to burn.

Speeding back down the state road toward town, the headlights show flickering glimpses of something large and gray on the shoulder, always just ahead of me, out of focus. But I know what it is: the God of the Screen is angry. But that's okay. So am I.

The world is again stretched and distorted by tracking lines. *He's in you already*, that's what Heather said. If that's true, he's in good company, slinking around with the Wolf Man and Godzilla and a horde of vampires, mutants, and masked killers. I've been dreaming of monsters my whole life. I've seen all the movies. I know what to do.

I drive through the dark, remembering how it feels to live a dream, why I loved the movies so much before it became a grind. Just a job. An easy way to meet easy women. I see why Dad never stopped. It can be a drug as powerful as any I ever found in L.A.—and I searched very thoroughly.

I'm Han Solo, coming back to cover Luke and see the Death Star explode.

I'm the Duke, sniping Liberty Valance from across the street.

I'm Rocky, still on his feet in the final round.

But then I'm just me again, a scared guy in a crappy Buick. It's tempting to hide in the comfy haze of nostalgia, to make our lives fit the stories we love. I've made a pretty decent living at it. But life has no end credits, no second takes. And remakes suck, almost always. I'm old enough to know that. I've paid my respects, but the old gods had their day.

Behind me, I see red and blue lights flashing. The sheriff must have been nearby the whole time, chaperoning my date with the pizza princess. An insurance policy, in case I didn't respond to sweet talk and seduction. Everybody speaks bullets. I can't outrun him, not in this heap. But that's okay too. I don't have far to go now. I never did.

I think maybe I've always been working my way back to the shop. A part of me never left. I don't know if torching it will have any real effect. I don't know if these people can be saved, if they deserve to be. Because in many ways things here are better than ever.

Not for Dad though, are they? Not for the girl in the barn either. Not for those missing kids, and who knows how many others? Nobody came to help them. Failing a better contender, it seems I turned out to be the hero of this strange little saga. It's a new role, against type for sure, but I'm getting comfortable with the idea.

Nearing the shop, I see the Mayberry filter fade. The grocery store's sign doesn't actually advertise a healthy sale at all. It's broken, missing most of the letters. The church windows are shattered—that was real, at least—but the houses are just as decrepit as I remembered. The yards are patches of weeds. The homeless shapes slump against crumbling walls. These special effects are cheap and actually pretty easy to spot if you know how to look.

I depress the cigarette lighter.

Did you see the truth too, Dad? I think it's a matter of taste, like a tolerance. Maybe our preferences made us harder to trick. It certainly made him harder to please, cranky old snob. Maybe he was saved by that snobbery? His standards were too sterling. And me? Well, I never minded a little squalor. High class, poor taste—our educated eyes imbued us with resilience to this, whatever it is. Not immunity, I think. Maybe we just know what we like.

If that thing is in my mind, he should be the one afraid. He should have already seen there was only one way this would end. Because maybe I was a lousy son, maybe I have squandered my talent, maybe I don't treat people very well, and I sure do hate a lot of things—not least among them myself. But I like a big dramatic ending. Just ask my last wife.

The lighter ejects.

I touch the glowing tip to the pile of tapes on the seat beside me. It goes up quickly, as I thought it would. On the floor is the booze, bottles uncapped, sloshing onto the carpet. Pedal to the floor, I aim the Buick at the large front window of the Video Realm. One hand on the door handle, I prepare to bail.

Hope this is as easy as the movies make it look.

I don't know what it takes to topple a god, even one grasping so tenuously to power as the God of the Screen. My occupation is the creation of myths. But I do know one thing: there's a California sunrise waiting for me on the other side of this nightmare.

If I die, I'm a tragic artist, gone too soon and awaiting rediscovery. They'll call me a genius.

And if I live, maybe it's not too late for me after all.

I do hate remakes. But sequels? Well, I like sequels. Redemption stories are what great cinema is made of. And if I live through this, mine will make one hell of a movie. My best work yet.

I think I'll play myself.

The Brief, Reluctant Retirement and Shocking Resurrection of Spooky Sophie

1.

The leather-clad vixen grinned behind rolling credits as Braiden dragged a finger through the slowly pooling blood and brought it to his mouth.

On his knees before the TV as *Spooky Sophie's Midnight Sin-ema* gave way to an insurance commercial, Braiden bent over the savaged corpse and fought down a gag. The taste was still disappointing, just as it had been with Mr. Suresh at the store, and his mother before that. But Braiden forced himself to taste again, knowing he'd eventually come to embrace his true nature. After all, he had all the time in the world now. He was an immortal killer. A vampire. *Nosferatu.*

Finally, he dropped the knife and walked out of the trailer, bowing badly at the middle on its short cinderblock legs, leaving PITT-TV's Halloween weekend movie marathon playing and the dead old woman lying on the floor.

He paused in the doorway, a pale and skeletal man of about 30 with long dark hair, who looked even skinnier inside his black leather trench coat, to watch Spooky Sophie pull a scroll from between her breasts, unroll it, and announce the upcoming film: Mario Bava's *Black Sunday.*

"This picture's leading lady may be named *Steele*, but I'm guessing after one look at her it's you fellas in the audience who will feel a little *stiff*." Sophie winked. "Anybody else suddenly in the mood for Italian?"

Braiden actually preferred *Black Sabbath* (at least that one had Boris Karloff) but he smiled, thinking of how sexy Sophie would look with her eyes wide, mouth stretched into a scream: the perfect victim. She was the only thing about Pennsylvania he'd miss. But the movies themselves didn't matter to him so much anymore, not like they used to. Everything would be different now. *He* would different. Movies were for those without dreams of their own.

In the dirty Durango idling at the end of the trailer's walkway, JT banged his big bald head against the steering wheel in time with Mastodon's *Blood Mountain.* He flashed devil horns with one pudgy hand as Braiden approached. Above, the clear blue sky had darkened, smell of impending rain weighting the air.

"On to New Orleans now? Let's get this show on the road."

"One last stop." Braiden slid into the SUV's back seat beside Emma, the duffle bags pressed between them, ignoring the girl's worried eyes. "I've got something to take care of first."

Emma turned to look out the rear window. Her mouth opened slightly, as if to say something. The new silver stud in her tongue glinted between painted black lips, and a few extra inches of creamy thigh snuck out from beneath her short skirt, ruffled fabric the color of blood on pavement.

JT noisily hawked up a loogie and spit out his window at a gang of boys riding bikes along the road, shouting as he drove away, "Happy Halloween, losers!"

The trailer park grew smaller in the rearview mirror, then disappeared.

"Did Granny yell at you?" Emma asked. In the months since they'd met, Emma's grandmother did almost nothing but yell at Braiden—except to yell *about* him. The old woman did not care for the strangely dressed man paying her teenage granddaughter so much attention, or the changes the girl made to her attitude and appearance under his influence, and wasn't shy about saying so. "Was she upset I'm going away with you?"

Braiden reached over the bags and slid a hand between Emma's legs. The metallic tang of blood was still thick on his tongue. He swallowed hard.

"She came around."

2.

In the end, nobody helped Sophie carry her coffin.

Despite having spent a decade as PITT-TV's most recognizable personality—with her final Halloween marathon still airing at that very moment—she may as well have been The Invisible Woman for all the attention the production crew paid to her pleas for assistance. She had no doubt Merton was behind this final indignity as well, comradery of the station staff being the last thing that petty pervert could take from her now.

Regardless, Spooky Sophie, TV's reigning First Lady of Fright, was forced to wrestle it—a gorgeous pink casket with bronze and lilac-toned finish, plush black velvet bedding and matching pillow—onto an equipment cart and wheel it into the parking lot through the studio's loading dock all by herself.

From the start, pink and black had been the color scheme of *Spooky Sophie's Midnight Sin-ema.* Her coffin was pink. She'd sat inside it, lounged atop it, and leaned against it in more than a thousand different ways while introducing hundreds of horror movies (of widely disparate quality) to audiences (of varying degrees of sobriety) throughout the broadcast region.

Sophie's trademark costume—over-the-knee heeled boots and bodysuit with a neckline that didn't so much plunge as plummet to unapologetic indecency, a not-exactly functional combo at the best of times and complete hinderance during the performance of manual labor (like moving a coffin)—was black.

Black leather, of course. All of it tight as teeth and far shinier.

Iconic as it might be, however, the ensemble was little protection against the drizzling rain and chill of the Pittsburgh evening into which she made her ignominious exit. Sophie realized too late she'd forgotten her cloak inside while rushing to move the coffin. The leather was instantly slick, her exposed skin painfully cold, as she trudged beneath the nuclear glow of lights suspended above the parking lot. Shivering, she tossed her head to clear sodden strands of long dark hair from her face.

Damn, Sophie thought, *I bet Elvira never had to deal with this bullshit.*

Perhaps, but Cassandra Peterson was also playing in a very different cultural sandbox. Horror hosts were a critically endangered species in the 21st century—practically extinct. And the world of broadcast TV had changed dramatically since *Elvira's Movie Macabre* went off the air. Everything today was cheaper, more rushed, and increasingly desperate.

About as desperate, Sophie mused, boots nearly slipping out from under her as she pushed the coffin into the bed of her pickup, *as a suddenly unemployed former weather girl who's getting further past 40 every day. Someone with little education and few marketable skills outside her continued ability to squeeze herself into the wardrobe of a much younger woman and recite with a straight face abominable puns and movie titles like* Weasels Rip My Flesh.

Truthfully, she hadn't even been the station's actual weather girl, just the pretty face hired to fill the role while their meteorologist was on maternity leave. The now-infamous breakdown of Creepy Carl, the previous horror host, left an unexpected opening. With no better prospects and her days of gainful employment numbered, Sophie dressed up and stepped in.

She closed the truck's tailgate and watched Merton Allen, owner and general manager of the station, bring his hands together in a dramatic slow clap and step from the shadows like a low-rent monster in the schlockier movies on her show. Water beaded and hurried to run off his fancy coat and greased hair, as if touching him reluctantly, against its will—much the way that Sophie expected everybody touched Merton.

"Thanks for the help," she said.

"I would have lent a hand, but I was caught up enjoying the view." Merton's eyes slid over her body and Sophie shivered—this time, not from the cold.

"Get your last look, creep."

"Grace in defeat." Merton ran a hand lightly over his hair. "And to think I came all the way out here to say *bon voyage.* The decision not to renew your contract was purely fiduciary, Sophie. We need to be as profitable as possible if we're going to attract a major buyer like Sinclair or ABC. This has nothing whatsoever to do with my personal feelings about you. In fact, I'd hoped that you might reconsider my offer and stick around. I could use a lady like you in several positions."

"You're unbelievable."

"I can't tell you how many women have said that to me."

"Because you can't count."

"I can count to five. And that's exactly how many minutes you have to get off studio property before I call security."

"Is this about the staff barbecue? Because of what I said after you got drunk and whipped out your little—"

"Make that two minutes." Merton turned on the heel of his loafer and walked away. "You're wasting time, Sophie. And I wouldn't think an unemployed woman your age had any to spare."

Dusk congealed into night. The laughing call of a crow rang out across the parking lot, harsh and mirthless. As if cued by some hack director, the drizzle became a deluge.

Sophie was dry and cozy in her apartment, about halfway through a bottle of red wine, sitting on the couch in her most comfortable pajamas and looking at herself on TV present *The Lurking Fear* when the doorbell rang.

She checked the peephole and allowed the human tornado that was Avery to assault the room unimpeded. Shoes were kicked off, a purse tossed onto the floor, disgorging its contents like the burst guts of roadkill. A six-pack of Yuengling in one hand, box of pizza in the other, Avery marched to the kitchen and began partaking of both in the time it took Sophie to close and lock the door.

"I appreciate you coming over, but I'm fine. Really."

Avery scowled, mouth full.

"Honestly," Sophie said, "no regrets."

Avery swallowed and reached for a second slice. She was a short young woman, arms covered in tattoos, unruly blonde hair dyed purple at the tips. They'd met several years ago, during Avery's internship at the studio, and bonded instantly over a shared love of slasher films and hatred of Merton—who'd predicably showed a disconcerting amount of interest in Avery.

Sophie retrieved her glass, hearing the rain continue outside. She pictured the downpour falling onto her truck with the casket still in the back. She had no idea where she might keep it. Maybe she could sell it? Spooky Sophie was no Elvira, but she wasn't totally without fans.

She thought of Creepy Carl. More than a decade the man had spent on the air, breaking his back to entertain people for chump change, only to end up as nothing more than a cruel joke. Was that to be her legacy as well?

The movie was suddenly interrupted by a news report. The woman on TV said Andrew Suresh, owner of a gas station in the nearby town of East Brady, had been found murdered in his store, victim of an apparent robbery. One employee, Braiden Darrow, was being sought by authorities as a person of interest. Above the reporter's shoulder appeared a photo of a pale, gaunt young man with stringy black hair and sunken eyes.

The reporter said, "According to police, Mr. Suresh's body reportedly showed signs of having been partially—"

"You got any of that white sprinkly cheese dust?" Avery rummaged noisily inside the refrigerator. "Never mind, found it. How about some ranch?" Her phone lit up on the counter, grinding out the opening chords to Rob Zombie's "Living Dead Girl."

Sophie drained her glass, turned away from the TV, and reached for the bottle of wine.

The only bump in the ladies' relationship had been a surprisingly heated disagreement about Rob Zombie's *Halloween* films. Avery thought them underappreciated works of subversive brilliance, while Sophie had no use for any installment that did not feature Jamie Lee Curtis. They'd reached an unspoken agreement to never again bring up the subject.

Avery quickly silenced the phone, finished her beer, and cracked open a second. "You still going to the blood drive?" She punctuated the query with a belch.

Sophie stopped refilling her glass. "Is that tonight?"

"It's always the night before Halloween."

"Damn, I totally forgot. Honestly, I don't think I'm up for it."

"You promised!"

"But I'm exhausted. I was fired today, remember? And I really don't want to put that outfit back on this late at night."

"Spooky Sophie has never missed a Halloween Midnight Blood Drive," Avery said. "Come on, it's for the children's hospital. You take pictures, sign autographs, let some dudes gawk at your tits, and we're out. It's not even 9:30 yet."

"Easy for a cool young kid like you to say." Sophie laid her forehead on the kitchen counter and groaned. "But I'm an old woman. Next month I'll be—actually, never mind how old I'll be. I had a terrible enough day already."

"I thought you were fine, remember?"

"How can I be fine when I've got no job?!"

"There are other jobs. You're just freaking out because you've got no script."

"What do you mean?"

Avery shook a blizzard of parmesan onto her pizza. "I mean, maybe you got a little too comfy being this fake character? And every week you got a script that clearly told you exactly what was going to happen, what you should say, what to expect. It wasn't hard work and you got to feel like a star. Face it, honey, you got spoiled."

Sophie drained her glass and filled it again. "Is this supposed to be cheering me up?"

"Yes," Avery said. "Because you *invented* Spooky Sophie, remember? You were about to be a jobless bimbo—no offense—then just made up a whole new career for yourself. The sexy costume, the fearless attitude, the *truly* awful jokes, that's all you! And you are awesome. And speaking of awesome," her tone was theatrically casual, the wink implied, "isn't Vince supposed to be there tonight?"

As usual, thinking of the handsome paramedic made Sophie's stomach tighten in a not-unpleasant manner. Her face suddenly warmed against the counter.

They'd had several flirtatious interactions in the past, and during last year's Halloween event Sophie distinctly recalled seeing the man's shirt ride up enough to reveal the bottom of a tattoo on his left side. She very much wanted to see the rest of it. Slowly, she raised her head and met Avery's smirk.

"God, am I too old to have a crush?"

"I'd heft my ancient ass out of a hospice bed for somebody that hot."

"I must remember to warn your boyfriend."

"Oh please, I love George. We're definitely getting married someday. Doesn't mean I can't have naughty thoughts about a guy like Vince. And he's a paramedic, Sophie—that's practically a firefighter! He's basically a sexy firefighter. Honestly, you have no choice but to show up tonight and seduce him for charity."

Through the open bedroom door, Sophie regarded the leather costume and boots, still lying where she'd tossed them, in a puddle of water on the floor beside the hamper. It wouldn't take much, she thought, to dry them off. Her hair, somehow, wasn't a total disaster. And it really wasn't all that late.

"Well," she said at last, "I suppose if it's for a good cause..."

3.

At the gas station, Emma waited in the car while JT filled the tank and Braiden went inside for supplies.

"Smokes and road beers!" JT brayed with laughter, then looked at Emma and stuck his tongue between two fingers.

Emma quickly turned away, took out her phone, and tried again to call her grandmother. Once more, nobody answered. There was no reason Granny wouldn't be home at this hour, no reason she wouldn't pick up. A vague fear Emma could not articulate, or perhaps did not want to, gnawed at her guts. *She can't hate Braiden that much.*

Emma knew what everyone thought of Braiden. He wasn't a bad guy though, just a little strange. And Emma *liked* that he was different. Braiden didn't constantly talk about football and trucks and deer hunting, like every other guy she knew. He read weird books and watched old movies. Emma knew if they went someplace where nobody knew Braiden—where people wouldn't keep judging him for past mistakes—if she could get him to channel that strangeness into something productive, everything would be okay. Maybe he could write a vampire book? Somebody had to get paid to think up that crazy horror stuff. Whatever he came up with, it couldn't be worse than *Twilight.*

Emma shoved headphones in her ears and turned up The Cure. Robert Smith singing "A Night Like This" filled her head while she cradled her phone and thought of trying her grandmother again.

But she didn't.

She was afraid nobody would answer.

Inside, Braiden watched the doughy clerk with a short beard and hipster glasses bag a six-pack of Iron City, cigarettes, and an assortment of junk food.

"Your total is $74.98."

Braiden locked eyes with him and focused his energy, felt the immense power radiating from his body. He exhaled slowly and said, "No, it's not."

"Yeah, I'm pretty sure it is."

"I'm pretty sure it's not." Braiden did not blink. He reached forward with his mind and flexed his will, manifesting the cosmic weight of centuries, vitality of the souls of those humans on whom he'd fed. He felt his body alight with astral fire.

Tapping a finger against the register's digital display, the clerk said, "Cash or card?"

The door chime sounded as JT came to stand beside Braiden. He grabbed a handful of beef jerky from a nearby display. "This too," he said, eyeing the plastic-wrapped magazines behind the counter. "You got *Tits & Tail* back there?"

"Do you guys have any money?"

"I used to be like you." Braiden leaned forward, drumming his long black nails on the counter. "I even worked in a place just like this. But I *ascended*. I'm a pilgrim on the midnight road. I've walked between the worlds."

"Great," the clerk said, "but in this world right here, your total is $74.98."

"I am eternal."

"You are stoned." It was not this particular clerk's first double shift and these were far from his first freaks. His eyes were mid-roll when Braiden took out Mr. Suresh's pistol, which the old guy had kept in the office and hadn't realized Braiden knew about, and in one smooth motion, for the second time in less than 24 hours, stood in a convenience store and shot a man in the chest.

A gory crater obliterated the faded *Fangoria* logo on the clerk's t-shirt. Blood and pieces of lung sprayed the wall of cigarettes behind him. "Goddamn!" JT laughed in the sudden silence as he scooped up their spoils. "Cleanup at the register, am I right? Let's get out of here."

As the clerk lay on the floor, twitching weakly and bleeding, Braiden looked up at the security camera mounted to the ceiling and waved.

"Such is the fate," he said, "of all mortals who dare to defy me."

4.

And just like that, it was midnight. Halloween was upon them, and Sophie was glad she'd come.

Word of her cancellation had spread online and lots of people at the blood drive were outraged. There was talk of a petition. Some volunteered to protest, others swore to boycott PITT-TV and their sponsors. There was even a hashtag: #standwithsophie. Apparently, it was trending.

Because of lousy weather, the event was held beneath a makeshift covering of hastily erected canopies on the football field of Romero High School. A special place was set up for Sophie, slightly away from the donor stations, with haybales, dangling rubber bats, and a big cauldron brimming with smoky dry ice.

This time, Avery helped move her coffin.

Sophie posed for pictures and signed autographs. Avery worked the crowd, kept the line moving, and ushered away the inappropriately enthusiastic fanboys. When there was finally a lull, Avery reached into her backpack and produced a stainless steel thermos of wine.

"You think of everything," Sophie said.

Avery nodded and looked over the costumed crowd. At a long table on the far side of the field, people perused a selection of items donated for the yearly raffle. The Romero Knight went clanging by in his cheap tarnished armor, wildly swinging a plastic sword. "Monster Mash" played from speakers placed at strategic locations.

"It's kind of pagan when you think about it," Avery said. "We gather annually in the early hours of All Hallows' Eve to revel, clad in costumes, and make an offering of blood in the hope of keeping children healthy. It's not *The Wicker Man*, but it's not that far a stretch."

Sophie laughed. "The potential for human sacrifice aside, thanks for pushing me to come. This is exactly what I needed tonight."

"No." Avery pointed to the nearer of the two ambulances parked on the sideline of the Astroturf field. "*That* is exactly what you need tonight."

Sophie saw Vince leaning against the vehicle, muscly arms crossed over his chest, looking back at her with a smile. When their eyes met, he waved. Feeling herself blush, Sophie waved back.

"Jesus, are you passing each other on your way to study hall?" Avery took the thermos from Sophie and playfully smacked her behind. "Get over there and jump his bones, bitch."

"I can't remember the last time I even flirted with somebody out of character, let alone did any bone-jumping."

"You can't host your life like it's some midnight movie," Avery said. "There's no script anymore, remember? It's Halloween and you are Spooky-freaking-Sophie. Tonight is the luckiest night of that beefcake's life—he just doesn't know it yet."

Avery watched as Sophie screwed up her courage and strode through the crowd toward the ambulance. Immediately, the couple's body language was promising and Avery settled in to enjoy the show.

Then, a skinny guy in a long black coat blocked her view.

———

Emma was distracted from the blood drive's festivities by her phone's insistent chiming. She stepped out of the flow of people and didn't notice Braiden and JT move on without her, confused as she was by the barrage of texts from her cousin.

She said Braiden was on TV.

Braiden was wanted by the police.

A man had been killed at the store where Braiden worked.

Nobody was answering the phone at Granny's place.

She wanted to know where Emma was *right now!!!*

Emma looked up, dazed. The unease squirming in her guts began to solidify into an almost painful anxiety. It should have been ludicrous, the idea of Braiden as a murderer. It should be infuriating, seeing him so quickly suspected of something awful just because he dressed in black and talked about vampires all the time. It should have been hilarious, but it wasn't.

Emma felt each heartbeat strike her eyes like a hammer. Dizzy, she looked around, but could not see Braiden or JT. She didn't recognize anybody, and the costumes didn't seem fun anymore. The eyes of every character were cruel. Even the unmasked faces hurrying past seemed to stretch and leer at her, nightmarish caricatures of human beings.

Emma no longer heard the music playing or rain beating on the tarps overhead. She could not feel her feet move over the stiff fake grass. The wall of bodies seemed to part slightly as she stumbled through the shifting mass—and then, finally, Emma saw somebody she recognized.

Spooky Sophie was talking with a handsome guy near an ambulance. The man looked familiar, but Emma could not recall where she'd see him before. And her curiosity was quickly washed away by a flood of relief as she weaved through the crowd. If anybody could help her, Emma was certain it was Spooky Sophie. Fear, after all, was that woman's specialty. Monsters, her stock-in-trade. She would know what to do.

———

"You make a better door than a window, fella."

Avery looked the man over. A musky unwashed smell drifted off him, and Avery thought he looked about as healthy as the body always discovered in the opening scene of a *CSI* episode. Dark eyes regarded her unblinkingly from behind long, greasy black hair, which fell over his face like a moth-eaten curtain in an old-timey haunted house.

"I have come to meet Sophie." He spoke so quietly that Avery had to (reluctantly) lean closer to make out his words. "I have journeyed a considerable distance to make her acquaintance."

"Yeah? Well, keep your pants on. She'll be right back. The lady's just taking a quick break, okay?"

"I can wait." A smile Avery did not like slithered across the man's face. "Until the stars collapse on themselves and the cities of man are crumbling ruins, I can wait. I have all the time in the world."

"Great," Avery said, inching slowly away. "Glad to hear it. Excuse me, will you?"

She moved to find a better vantage point from which to observe Sophie's seduction of the paramedic—and possibly find a security guard. The long-haired guy was scary in a more-than-usual way. She could feel his haunting eyes burn into her back as she left, longing suddenly for the handsy fanboys.

That kind of creep, she could handle.

———

He stood where the little blonde left him, beside Spooky Sophie's coffin. It could not possibly be a coincidence, Braiden thought, both Sophie and his brother being at the same place at the same time. The universe was already reshaping itself in accordance with his will. It was better than a movie, better than he ever imagined. Sophie and Vincent—the perfect victim and ideal villain. His mouth practically watered.

This time, it would be delicious.

"I don't see him," JT whined between bites of a giant Hershey bar. "Can we go now?"

"No." Braiden scanned the crowd. "Not until I find Vincent."

"And Emma," JT said. "Now that silly bitch is missing too."

"Vincent isn't missing, I know he's here someplace. And if you insult my concubine once more, I'll hurt you."

"Whatever, man. Here you are waiting to meet this TV *chick*, the other *chick* ran off somewhere, and now there's no sign of Vince. This is getting boring, bro! I'm not your sidekick and I'm sick of taking orders. Just because you're finally getting some, that doesn't make you the boss of me. How about I go to New Orleans by myself?"

Braiden regarded his friend with a smile about as real as the bosom of the mustachioed Dolly Parton stumbling past on precipitous heels. "You got lost driving downtown for Comic-Con, dipshit. Really think you can find New Orleans without me? And when you get there, what will you do? You don't know anybody."

"Neither do you."

"I know where to go. There are secret places where my kind gather."

"Your kind? Please, save that *Queen of the Damned* crap for your chick, man. I've known you too long."

"I'm beginning to find you tiresome, JT."

"I wish you'd start finding your brother already."

"Vincent cannot hide forever. Soon, I'll locate—"

"He's right there, Dracula." JT pointed at a nearby ambulance.

Braiden's eyes narrowed as he beheld his brother, wearing no coat over his tight EMS t-shirt despite the cold, trying to look like he wasn't flexing his ridiculous muscles and standing very close to Spooky Sophie.

Her costume was shiny and tight, exposed flesh enticingly damp from the rain. He watched as she threw back her head and laughed, teeth white and straight, neck slender and gloriously pale. Braiden imagined the hot blood coursing just below her skin and licked his lips. Yes, with her it would be different. The taste as glorious as he'd always hoped.

"Looks like Vince already has dibs on your precious TV chick," JT said.

Sophie and Vincent turned as an obviously upset Emma approached. Her large eyes were brimming with tears. She gestured emphatically, said something Braiden could not hear. The music was loud, noise of the crowd an incomprehensible drone. He watched his older brother reach out and put a hand on Emma's shoulder, his own closing simultaneously around the gun in his pocket.

JT laughed and stuffed the rest of the candy bar into his mouth.

"Looks like he's got both of them!"

5.

Vince's demeanor changed immediately when the long-haired creep appeared.

One minute, the world was full of happy people shuffling, stumbling, and dancing around them, same as before. Then came the crying girl, and right away Vince was calm and in control, comforting the kid and making sense of things. Sophie was already thinking of how they might tell this strange story later, seeing the memory as if it were a scene in one of the movies on her show.

Then, out of nowhere, the pale guy was just *there*, as if by magic. Hands in the pockets of his long black coat, he stood regarding her, Vince, and the girl with a strange expression. He seemed happy, sort of, but also angry. It was the same way Merton smiled watching her load the coffin into her truck.

"Braiden?" Vince asked. "What the hell are you doing here? The police came to my apartment looking for you. They want to talk about some robbery where you work. Do you know anything about that? They said nobody answered the door at mom's place. And when I called, she never picked up."

"Mother's a little buried at the moment."

"What the hell does that mean?"

"Think hard, Vincent. But try not to hurt yourself."

At that moment, Emma recognized Vince, having seen his picture at the house where Braiden lived with his mother. With that realization, everything Braiden said that night, the true implications of his words, came back to her.

"Braiden," she whispered, "what did you do?"

"Wait, *this* is your boyfriend?" Vince jerked a thumb at his brother. "*This* is the guy you're so afraid of?"

"Fear is the only rational response left for you now, Vincent," Braiden said, still smiling. "I've put things in motion you cannot possibly comprehend. Tonight, I begin remaking the world. My dreadful dynasty is nigh. But first I've come to give you this one chance. To show I'm not completely without mercy."

"What the actual fuck are you talking about?"

"I've come to give you the opportunity to apologize. For all the indignities you inflicted on me before I was reborn into darkness. If you fall to your knees right now and beg my pardon, I promise to make it quick."

Vincent stepped forward and shoved his brother, nearly knocking Braiden to the ground and bringing, for the briefest flash of a second, a look of fear to his pale, gaunt face.

"Make *what* quick, you creepy little geek?"

Braiden pulled out the pistol and trained it on his brother.

"Your execution."

Emma screamed.

She wasn't the only one.

Instantly, people rushed away on every side. Somebody tripped over a wire and the music was abruptly silenced. The Romero Knight lay spreadeagle on the sideline, sword still in hand, unable (or unwilling) to stand up again.

Braiden winked at Sophie and bared his teeth. "I'll get to you next, sweetheart. Big fan, by the way. But really, *Black Sunday* instead of *Black Sabbath*? What were you thinking?"

"I don't pick the movies." Sophie didn't recognize her own voice. "The producers... They tell me what to do."

"I've got some things for you to do. And if you do them really well, I might even let you live to tell the tale."

Sophie looked for a cop, a security guard, somebody—anybody!— to come and take charge of the situation, as Vince had been doing moments (already it felt like eons) ago. In this part of the movie, somebody always charged in to fight the monster and save the day. It didn't make sense.

"Braiden, you need to stop this right now." Vince took a tentative step toward his brother, hands halfway raised.

The gun's aim did not waver. "You sound just like Mr. Suresh. Just like Mom. And Emma's stupid grandmother. I hoped you might rise to the occasion, Vincent. Be wise enough to see the privilege I'm granting you."

From the makeshift shelter of stacked haybales, overturned tables, and from behind the ambulance, Sophie saw trembling hands cradling cellphones, the cold unblinking eyes of their camera lenses watching the surreal scene in which she found herself a reluctant star.

An overweight bald guy, who looked a bit like an actor Sophie could not immediately name, broke the trend and stalked forward, the look on his face more fury than fear.

"Dude," JT said, "what are you doing? Let's go already."

Braiden looked from Vince to Sophie to Emma. His eyes were blank, shattered windows in an abandoned building. "I've got everything I want right here."

"Come on, man," JT said. "Let's get this show on the road."

Braiden pointed the gun at his friend. "Don't defy me."

"Dude," JT's voice was tired and sad, "you're not really a—"

The top section of the JT's head exploded in a shower of wet red gore, fragments of bone and teeth. His tongue flopped within the suddenly exposed crater of his jaw like a freshly caught fish, while his nearly decapitated body slumped slowly, almost gracefully, to its knees, then toppled over.

Vince took a big step back, his handsome face the color of snow in a black-and-white movie.

Emma covered her eyes with both hands.

Sophie thought the wound looked fake, like cheap made-for-TV effects, and tried again to decide which actor the bald guy reminded her of.

"I am Nosferatu!" Braiden shrieked at the cowering audience, becoming more unhinged, his voice growing louder and more shrill with each declaration. "I've tasted the blood of kings! I've seen the darkness behind the sun! I'm immortal, you morons, and I'm fucking ascendant!"

He snatched up from the ground a bulging bag of blood and tore it open with his teeth. Laughing hysterically, Braiden raised the bag over his head and poured the still-warm contents into his gaping mouth, splashing blood over his face and soaking the front of his shirt.

Almost instantly, he retched

Braiden's eyes went wide as he let loose a violent spew of discolored blood, bile, and half-digested junk food. Dazedly, as if somehow confused about what was happening to him, he glanced down at his ruined clothes, the gruesome puddle at his feet. Then, he slowly looked at Vince, Emma, and the silently recording cameras.

Just for a moment, it seemed as if he might cry.

Then, Braiden found Sophie and seemed to become sure of himself again—or sure of *something*, at least. Something only he understood, perhaps. Braiden blew Sophie a little kiss with bloody lips. His ghastly smile, as he slowly raised the pistol, was an atrocity.

At that moment, Vince rushed his distracted brother. They collided and began to struggle. Twice, the gun went off, bullets speeding upward through the tarp, disappearing into the stormy black sky above.

All the old instincts reared up and Sophie had to chew her lip to keep from quipping some nonsense about what a *grave* situation it was. A shout drew her attention to where Avery had climbed atop a pile of haybales. The tiny blonde called out as she hurled the weighty thermos. "Pretend he's Malcolm McDowell in *Halloween II!*"

Sophie moved to catch it, a strange new fury growing in her heart, thinking, *There's only one* Halloween II, *and Malcolm McDowell is NOT in it!*

The pistol went skidding away from the wrestling figures. Braiden, screaming furiously, drove the long black nails of his thumbs into both his brother's eyes.

That's a great Fulci homage, Sophie thought—then caught herself. *What's wrong with me? This is not a movie.*

She forced herself forward, feeling the comfortingly real weight of the thermos in her hands. The wine was real, she knew that for sure—so was Avery, so was Vince. And that meant the blood and horror she'd seen tonight were real. She could not be some sexy prop. She could not remain a witness, lounging on the sideline, preening and posing and cracking wise from the safety of her coffin. This time, there was no script.

It's Halloween night, she thought. *And I am Spooky-freaking-Sophie.*

Avery's words came back to her like a dramatic (and thematically unnecessary) voiceover: *You can't host your life like it's some midnight movie.* Because she wasn't a host anymore. She'd been fired from that gig. This time, like it or not, Sophie was a character.

Vince wailed, grabbed his brother's wrists, and wrenched Braiden's hands away before rolling aside, tears of blood trickling down his face.

Braiden scrambled to his feet and sucked the gore from his thumb.

Sophie thought about Merton Allen and Creepy Carl, Boris Karloff and Barbara Steele. She thought about Elvira and Vampira. She thought about Jamie Lee Curtis, and even spared a moment's compassion for Rob Zombie, as she stood behind the lunatic in black and raised the heavy thermos.

"Such is the fate," Braiden said, "of all mortals who dare—"

The stainless steel made a loud and satisfying *crack* as it struck Braiden's face, a geyser of blood erupting from his smashed nose as Sophie watched him collapse faster than an Ed Wood set.

Braiden hissed something unintelligible through the blood and broken teeth. But it sounded like he'd called her a not-nice word, so Sophie went ahead and hit him again, just to be safe.

Even as Braiden reached a state of humiliation and agony he previously would have been unable to imagine, a small part of him, furiously enough, managed to register that he still found the taste of blood unpleasant; even his own. Nothing had felt as he'd imagined it would. He reached forward with his mind, flexing his will and manifesting the cosmic weight of centuries as—

Sophie drove her foot into Braiden's stomach.

He rolled into a quivering ball and cried out as she stomped down hard, seeming to make a point of leading with the sharp heel of her boot. Blood splashed onto the black leather of her costume like something out of a Dario Argento wet dream.

The pained whimpering of Braiden and Vince was drowned out by a strange new sound, but Sophie heard only the impact of each blow striking the cowering creature at her feet. It was not until later, when she watched the videos posted online, that she realized she'd been screaming.

Finally, breathing hard, sweat chilling on her skin in the cold darkness of the early Halloween morning, Sophie wiped a strand of long black hair from her face and said, "You are the worst thing to happen to vampires since Stephenie Meyer."

Braiden watched Sophie's boot descend again, the sole looming larger than the asteroid that killed the dinosaurs. A true catastrophe. An *Armageddon* even Bruce Willis couldn't prevent. Somewhere far away, people cheered—or did they scream? He smiled (as best his savaged mouth could manage) and pictured scores of horrified faces turned upward, pleading. He had not been defeated, Braiden thought.

No, it was merely the end of the world, that was all.

And good riddance to it.

6.

"That concludes our examination of *The Amityville Horror* franchise and wraps up the 25th episode—can you believe we've been doing this for six months already?—of *Spooky Sophie's Midnight Podcast*. I'll be at Dark Culture Con in Memphis in two weeks and Creep Con in Knoxville after that. I want to thank everybody for listening and supporting the show. Be sure to like and subscribe and follow in all the usual places. Before I hand things over to Evil Emma, our Infernal Intern, for some listener mail, I'm getting the finger from the World's Sexiest Producer, which can only mean one thing: Breaking News Alert! What's up, Avery?"

"I've just received an update about our favorite human dumpster fire: Count *Dick*-ula."

"*Fang*-tastic, I'm all ears."

"Seems Braiden Darrow's lawyer has petitioned for his next court appearance to be delayed because his client's jaw allegedly remains wired shut, meaning the poor little psycho cannot properly testify on his own behalf."

"A vampire with a broken jaw? Must be a real pain in the neck."

"Ha! Cue the rimshot."

"Well, Emma, you knew him best. What do you think?"

"I guess maybe the lawyer has a point—you have to admit, there's a lot at *stake*."

"Oh, God."

"Nice! Then again, that guy may have *arterial* motives of his own."

"Sophie, that was painful. Even for you."

"What can I say? I'm the kind of gal who appreciates *bat* jokes."

"That's it, I quit."

"Come on, Avery! I told that one to Vince the other night and he laughed so hard he started *coffin*."

"Men will laugh at anything said by a pretty lady sitting on their lap. Just be glad the doctors saved his eyes, because your sense of humor needs all the help it can get."

"Our subscription numbers say otherwise. Spooky Sophie is an oral phenomenon!"

"I think I read that on the wall in a truck stop bathroom."

"Yes, you did—because I wrote it there! No such thing as bad press, baby! Be sure to join us next week, listeners, when our special guest will be a local horror hero who needs no introduction: Pittsburgh's own Creepy Carl! Recently resurrected by popular demand and proving quite a hit on the convention circuit, Carl and I will talk about the pitfalls of celebrity, his favorite scary movies, and the tragically real horrors of working in broadcast TV. One podcast, two horror hosts. Don't miss it!"

Black Dog Blues

Choosing sides; that's what you're doing when you tell a story like this.

By clearly identifying the aberrant, we define and agree upon what is normal. We share unusual experiences and observations and thus reassure each other. It's practically ritualistic, a way of definitively declaring that *that* is not right, and we are not *that*, so therefore we are right. You understand?

That can be whatever—ghosts, monsters, the Bermuda Triangle, flying saucers filled with little green men—it doesn't matter. But such stories need to be shared. The point of telling tall tales is to recalibrate reality, and we truckers tell 'em taller than most.

You got your seatbelt on? Good deal.

As I was saying, culture is full of tribes, little clubs, and cults. Most of them have distinctive codes and traditions, their own myths and legends. I was in the Navy for about ten years and can tell you that sailors are an especially insular lot. I've known plenty of cops too, a members-only club if there ever was one. I imagine it's the same all over if you dig deep enough.

And truckers? Well, maybe we need the psychological anchoring sharing such stories provides more than most because ours is such an unnatural way to live. There's a reason the species, by and large, gave up the nomadic way of life a long time ago: it wears on you! I should know, been behind the wheel going on thirty years, crisscrossed this great big country more times than I can count. I have seen things you would not believe, trust me.

That vent blowing on you too much? I can adjust the heat. This rig has so many buttons, dials, and settings it's like a submarine or space ship. Actually, with all the glowing indicators and instruments up here, late at night when it's just me and the slim path cut by the headlights against all that dark, I sometimes feel like I'm driving through outer space. Like I'm out here all alone, hurtling through the void.

You okay then? Good deal.

That's why I picked you up. I don't usually give rides, but I know how cold it gets out here when the sun goes away. Plus, sometimes a little company, somebody to talk to, especially at night, it makes the miles go faster. You've got music if you want, and the CB radio, but those distant crackly voices can sometimes make a man feel more lonely rather than less. Sound kind of like ghosts, I think. People talking to you from...someplace else.

Which brings me back to what I started to say. Took the long way 'round the reservation on that one, sorry about that. But I promised you a story and I always keep my promises, ask anybody you like. They don't call me True Blue for nothing. True Blue being my radio handle; every trucker worth his wipers has one.

Now, consider the glow of the dials and panels, the gentle crackle and hiss of the CB. Not so dissimilar from a campfire, right? It's the perfect setting for the aforementioned ritual of recounting the so-called ghost story. Truckers have quite a stable of yarns to select from, but of all the legends traded amongst the tribe of professional drivers—sailors of the asphalt sea, you might say—the black dog is unquestionably the most iconic. Think there was even a movie made about it. Starred Meat Loaf, Randy Travis, and the guy from that dancing movie. Remember? *Nobody puts Baby in a corner?* Hell, it'll come to me.

The dog—more like a wolf, really—is an enormous, loping, slavering beast. Teeth, big as kitchen knives. Hair, black as space without stars. Eyes that blaze fiery red like emergency flares on a lonely stretch of bad road.

They say a driver who's been awake too long sees it just before a crash—the type you don't walk away from. Does the dog cause the crash? Maybe it's trying to warn you. There are many variations. Back when I was coming up, the old-timers said it comes to carry off your soul afterward, like a spirit guide in some Indian vision quest. But I don't believe that. It's no simple omen either, not the hallucination of a tired mind. The dog is very, very real. Every driver only has so many miles in them. And then, when you're coming to the end, that's when you see it.

First, the dog paces you, racing alongside the rig. The driver gets scared and goes faster, trying to lose it. He's heard the stories, after all, but thinks maybe he can outrun the thing. Maybe it's not too late. And for a minute or so, seems he's right. It's gone, vanished into the rushing darkness. That's when you see it again, barreling out of the night ahead. Its roar is squealing brakes and twisting metal, breath like burnt rubber and oily smoke.

You still okay? Good deal.

If you're fading, help yourself to those red pills in the far cup holder. Careful though, they're serious stuff. Speaking of which, pass me a few. This is no time to lose your edge. Miles to go and all that, right? Thanks.

There's coffee in that blue thermos and a can or two of cola in the fridge behind your seat. I tell you, these new rigs are really something. All these gizmos and creature comforts. You'd never know we're creeping past eighty because the ride's so smooth. Don't worry, I'm a professional. And like a wise man once said: I never drive faster than I can see.

Now then, I first obtained the facts regarding the black dog from a most reliable source, the man who taught me the ways of the wheel. Sullivan Smith drove for a cross-country outfit for about two hundred years before moving onto a local route near the shipyard in Bremerton, where I got out of the Navy. I was hired on as a probie and he was my training instructor. Geezer's handle was Locksmith because he'd supposedly been something of a Don Juan back in the Pleistocene Epoch. Had the key to the heart of every lady he met, or so they say.

He told me all about the black dog and I sat there nodding politely, just like you, and thinking pretty much what I expect you're thinking right now. It took a long time before I understood the truth.

Locksmith died about sixteen years ago, but not in a crash. Gas station robbery. Poor old man walked into an all-nighter for a doughnut and a cup of coffee, right into a holdup. Got the back of his head blown off by some desperate junkie with a shotgun before he knew anything was up. Actually not a bad way to go, if you think about it. I've seen worse. Yes, I certainly have.

It was Locksmith who first told me about the music, though I've heard others mention it since. Black Dog Blues, he called it. The sound a driver hears just before the dog appears, a sorrowful howling that leaks through on the CB and sharp, staticky barking. Sometimes, they say, you'll hear an inhuman voice growl your name. That's how you'll know it's time.

You've got your belt on, right? Good deal.

I heard the Black Dog Blues once, except it wasn't playing for me. There was this woman, a trucker, name was Lydia but her handle was Sassy because she had one hell of a smart mouth. Never cared who might be listening, right there on the CB she'd just say whatever she was thinking. We used to stop at the same spots and run the same routes. There are drivers who work in teams—partners, married couples; it gets awful lonely out here—and we were talking about maybe giving that kind of arrangement a try. Never got the chance though.

We were both slated to make a run for the same outfit. I'd gotten this new radar detector, so I was driving point and keeping an eye out for Smokies. We were making good time and chatting on the CB, us two and a few others in the general area, playing this game where we'd be carrying on a technically PG-rated conversation but using as many sexual innuendos and double entendres as possible. Sassy was good at it. Sometimes, I'd get to laughing so hard I couldn't breathe.

I said we were making good time. In fact, we were speeding along pretty well. That was the whole point of the radar detector. But the thing started acting funny, making crazy chirps and beeps, and I got distracted trying to restart it. I didn't notice Sassy had stopped talking. I didn't notice anything until I saw her rig bearing down on me, coming up way too fast on the left. Brake failure, I assumed. Something had to be wrong with the rig because Sassy was an outstanding driver. I was cruising just below the century mark—about how fast we're going now, actually—and she flew past me like I was parked.

That's when I saw it, just for a second as she passed, running outside the beam of her lights. An enormous black dog moving unbelievably fast. I got on the CB, but she didn't answer. So I pulled out my phone and called her. She did answer then, and I heard her crying. She was so afraid, kept screaming, "It's coming for me, True! It's coming for me!"

And in the background I heard her CB crackling. This awful howl, a scream of static that hurt my ears. It wasn't coming through on my radio though. I could only hear it on the phone. It was the Black Dog Blues playing just for her.

Something said her name. A voice like out of your worst nightmare. If there is a Hell, I think whatever greets you at the gates will sound like that. I saw her rig jackknife and go careening off the road. Thing rolled three times as it went over the embankment. By the time I finally got slowed down, pulled over, and ran back to the scene, the fire was so big...there was nothing I could... She was just gone.

That was three weeks ago. I've racked up a lot of miles since then. Side gigs, overtime—I don't like to stay put too long. Figure I've been up about four days straight now. Pardon my reach, just need something out of the glove compartment. Relax, it isn't for you.

This is the Smith & Wesson Governor, a snub-nosed revolver capable of firing small-caliber shotgun shells. A very reliable gun. Please don't look at me like that. I already told you, I'm a professional. The gun is for the dog. The story, that's for you. Like I said, such stories need to be shared. Make sure you got your belt on now. I'm counting on you to survive this and tell the tale. Please, be on my side.

You mean you really haven't seen it? On the shoulder of the road, just outside the headlights? Running alongside the rig? Right there! You can't see that?

No, too late. It's gone...for now.

Never mind, I'm not too worried about it. Let's coax this big boy up to a buck-twenty and see if we can't run the bastard down. Keep your eyes peeled. Somewhere in that blackness up there, it's headed straight for us. And I'm going to kill it. They didn't believe me when I told them what happened to Sassy. Looked at me like I was a raving lunatic. About like how you're looking at me right now, actually. But that's okay. I don't care what they think—or you either, matter of fact. Soon you'll see for yourself. Then you'll know the truth. And you can tell everybody. You can tell the story.

Hear that? It's as if the sound was being stretched and pulled like taffy, and that terrible crackling growl under the static. That howling, lonesome as a lifetime spent on the road.

Oh yes, they're playing my song tonight.

My Eyes Are Closed to Your Light

An underlying stink of mildew needled through the oppressive slathering of lemon-scented something. The carpet was the color of an unimaginative child's muddled fingerpainting. Lighting, weak and jaundiced. Temperature, frigid and somehow simultaneously muggy.

Yes, Stacey thought, this sad dingy place was the perfect spot for the crazy bastard to end up. He couldn't have written it any better.

Corrington Manor had most likely been exactly the sort of high-end rustic retreat still vaguely conjured, when seen in the right light, by the faded sagging remains of the large country inn. But if so, that time had been long before she and Elisabeth showed up. Before Kane Stryker chose it as the location where he was, in police parlance, *last positively identified* nearly six months ago.

That being said, it was objectively the ideal vanishing point for a man who'd spent much of his life writing about just such lonesome rural abodes and the terrible things that often lurk there. Even the weather had so far been something out of Stryker's sordid stories. The sky, ash-gray at its brightest, darkened swiftly just after lunch. And rain beat continuously against the windows on the other side of the room's cheap wine-maroon curtains since their arrival. It sounded like a billion tiny fists begging entry.

Stacey sat cross-legged on one of the room's twin beds. She read, rearranged the many pages spread before her, and read on, thoughtlessly brushing curly black hair from her eyes, teeth absently adding new chew marks to her already thoroughly gnawed pencil. She'd spent countless hours forcing Stryker's chaotic intellectual remains into some semblance of order, but even now they remained maddeningly semi-coherent at best. Manic dispatches from his increasingly long forays into a hellish alternate reality, one which had apparently consumed him at last.

Elisabeth sighed loudly, drawing Stacey's focus reluctantly from the ocean of paper. She lay on her stomach on the other bed, and, despite the chill, wore only a white t-shirt and black panties. She languidly kicked her feet in that way that made her athletic thighs and ass flex perfectly—the way she did when she wanted attention.

"Yes?" Stacey said.

"I'm sorry." Elisabeth looked up with exaggerated innocence. "Did you say something?"

"I can literally feel you seething over there."

"And I can literally hear your brain cells burning up." Elisabeth rolled over, threw one forearm dramatically over her eyes. "Can we please get out of here for just like an hour? You need a break and I am losing it."

"I told you not to come." Stacey returned to the manuscript. "When the rain stops, I'm going to the graveyard. I'm almost certain that's the place he was writing about. Tag along if you want."

"Well," Elisabeth said, "let's at least go wait it out in that bar down the hill. Come on, he for sure went in for a pint or twenty while he was here, the fucking lush. It's totally related to your thing in like a corresponding way."

"You mean in a *supporting* way? As in a *supporting source*? Didn't you major in communications?"

"Multimedia communications," Elisabeth said. "I don't do fancy terminology. But fine then, English Lit, in a *supporting* way. Now let's get buzzed in the dive where your nutcase hero almost definitely tried to drown his crazy ass in cheap beer."

No doubt she was right about the pub. Someone there could know something, something that would shed light on Stryker's cryptic clues, but had meant nothing to the cops, that didn't make it into their reports. And a break did sound wonderful just then; her brain was fuzzy and her eyes burned. But Stacey was still unable to resist one more poke.

"He drinks bourbon."

"He *drank* bourbon," Elisabeth said. Accustomed as she was to getting her way, she'd taken even that little engagement as acquiescence, excitedly rolling off the bed, snatching her jeans from the adjacent armchair and tugging them on. "And I would drink a Listerine margarita to get out of this room for even just thirty fucking minutes."

The pub was all aged wood and rough stone, decorated with rusty saw blades and the heads of mounted beasts. At a pinewood table near the long fireplace, blazing brightly and cheerfully enough to cauterize the tension they'd brought down with them from Corrington Manor—all the way from Nashville, really—their hair and clothes dried as they drank glasses of ale, dark and icy as the night outside.

Elisabeth drew the usual stares from the few elderly men huddled at the bar. She was a showstopper: tall, thick in all the right places, and unapologetically flirtatious. She always knew how she looked, and she always looked good. Upon removing her jacket, her long wet blonde hair quickly soaked the thin t-shirt and she was, assertive nipples and all, unashamedly giving the gawking geezers a show the likes of which they hadn't seen in many presidential elections.

Embarrassed at first, by the first sip of the third round Stacey was enjoying the spectacle too, even as the cotton dried and Elisabeth turned their talk to a more serious subject.

"What are we doing here?"

The tone was familiar, a reflexive disdain for anything that didn't immediately interest her. Stacey genuinely feared that tone back when they were students in Knoxville. She'd feared anything that might possibly upset Elisabeth then, when they lived on the same floor of a ratty apartment building and she'd been awkward and shy, and Elisabeth, beautiful bold Elisabeth, had somehow—impossibly—actually been into her.

Back then she'd lived around studiously avoiding anything that inspired that tone—movies, music, interests, clothes. She was a good student too, and had almost forgotten what it sounded like. But with the benefit of time passing, Stacey had begun to suspect her slavish devotion was almost certainly what attracted Elisabeth to her most. It was an unpleasant hunch slowly proven true with the prompt return of that tone whenever Stacey busied herself with something other than pleasing Elisabeth, who could not stand being more than an arm's length from the center of attention. She loathed being left out almost as much as she hated Stryker, and as such, this outing was something of a perfect cocktail of bitterly painful ingredients.

A short but intense entanglement with the man back in her student days had since led Stacey—with Elisabeth reluctantly and very outspokenly in tow—through a tumultuous correspondence, then the piecemeal maelstrom of his final writings, and finally to miles-from-nowhere, Tennessee. The creepy Corrington Manor. And the graveyard on the hill.

To the end, hopefully.

"Please," Elisabeth took Stacey's hand, "just tell me what you want from this exactly."

Stacey eyed the fire. "The book," she said at last. "It needs an ending."

"That pile of lunatic scribbles you've got back in the room? Babe, please, that's not a book. It's a manifesto at best." Elisabeth drained her beer and raised the empty glass to signal the bartender. She was not enduring any more of this trip sober if she could help it.

"Not *his* book," Stacey said. "The book I'm going to write about him. Look, I know he was using me. For longer than I care to admit, he was using me. But now I'm using him, all right? We graduated almost five years ago, Liz. I'm sick of writing clickbait and bullshit listicles. I was supposed to be so much further along by now."

"You're doing fine," Elisabeth said. "Everyone our age struggles."

Easy for her to say, Stacey thought. Just like everything was easy for Liz. Dismissing her feelings was prudent too. Unhappy people make changes. And what does an already revered goddess aspire to? More of the same, of course.

"I'm sick of struggling." Stacey swirled the dregs of her drink and downed it quickly. She did not have Elisabeth's tolerance and the alcohol was going to her head, loosening her tongue. But Liz long since made it clear she didn't like drinking alone, so Stacey obediently kept pace, already feeling the hangover looming. "A book about Stryker will sell, I know it. And there's nobody who could write it like me, nobody he was closer to by the end. I'll use his name to make people take mine seriously."

The bartender, fat and bald in a thick flannel shirt, set two fresh beers on the table and retrieved their empty glasses. He stared dumbly for a minute, then slowly backed away, as if afraid to turn his back on them.

"I'm not sure what makes these ol' fellers more uncomfortable," Elisabeth drawled. "Seeing my braless breasts in here—seeing any breasts in here, probably—or the fact that they're sitting just a little too close to your sexy little ass."

"The latter," Stacey said. "Definitely."

"Well, let's go see if we can put them at ease." Elisabeth stood, grinning wickedly.

"What are you doing?"

"Come on." Elisabeth grabbed their drinks. "You want to ask about Stryker, right? Well, those guys look like they live in here. If it's important to you, let's do it. You know I can turn on the charm." She made her eyes big, her voice breathy and low as she chewed her lip. "Gee, mister, I'd sure be ever so grateful if you'd tell my friend here all about that guy. Please?"

Stacey beamed and got to her feet. "Thanks, Liz."

Elisabeth winked. "You can thank me later, back in the room."

———————

Laughing, they climbed the hill, assaulted by rain that definitely hadn't let up. Stacey's shelling out for a few rounds had done far more than Elisabeth's breasts and feminine wiles to loosen the lips of the locals (a humbling revelation Elisabeth was actively ignoring). Not that they'd learned much anyway, nothing that wasn't in the police reports. Stacey wasn't surprised. Stryker had never been one for making friends, nor much opposed to drinking alone.

Still, seeing Elisabeth doing something for her for a change was wonderful. Though it did drive home just how rare an occurrence it was. She'd lit up the room, as always, and gotten what there was to get from the men. That it amounted to nothing was not her fault.

Elisabeth clapped a hand on Stacey's shoulder, and in a perfect imitation of the bartender's gruff voice said, "So y'all are...roommates?"

They broke up again, laughing.

"And then," Elisabeth managed, "when I said we were sisters? Did you see his face?"

"Y'all mean like *sorority* sisters?"

They burst wet, drunk, and noisy into the manor lobby, self-conscious in the quiet even though there didn't appear to be any other guests to disturb. Stacey's little white pickup was still alone in the parking lot. Giggling, they scurried down the otherwise silent hall to their room.

Inside, Stacey stood wet and shivering as Elisabeth fumbled about blindly in the dark unfamiliar space looking for the light switch. Somewhere far below, the ancient furnace came to life and the room was filled with the clanking and rattling of its efforts. For just a moment, Stacey was adrift in time and space, floating in an inky cacophonous void.

And then she was back in the pub, reliving the moment she'd gone to the bar to settle their tab while Elisabeth enjoyed a brief moment of fawning by the locals. She'd found herself beside a man, oldest of the crowd and the only one completely oblivious to Elisabeth's spectacle. The furnace noises became the choked wheezing of his sickly breath. The blackness was almost as dark as his eyes, staring intently back at her from his stool.

He was painfully thin, with gnarled reptilian hands curled protectively around his glass. Anxiety rising, drink making her heartbeat sound very loud inside her head, she'd groped for something to say, anything she could put between herself and that stare. As his noisy breath and the wolfish laughter of the men circling Elisabeth grew louder, Stacey at last blurted something about looking forward to visiting the cemetery.

"S'full," he slurred. "Always been there. Always been full. Nobody buried up there since 'fore I was born."

"Oh, is that right?"

The bartender seemed unable to count change. The noises of the men were more animalistic all the time. The old guy nodded slowly.

"That feller you's looking for, he asked 'bout it too."

She froze. It was the first time anyone in the bar said more about Stryker than simply admitting he'd stopped in, that he drank whiskey in lonely silence. *She'd been right.*

"Ain't nothing good up there," the man said into his glass. "Told him so. I'm telling you the same."

An explosion of light and Stacey was yanked back to reality, the feel of hands groping her. She blinked hard, trying to force the world into focus, but it continued swaying treacherously. She was drunker than she'd realized.

"Come on," Elisabeth said, "let's get you out of these wet clothes."

Stacey obediently raised her arms and Elisabeth pulled off her shirt. "I'm going to the cemetery." Her tongue was thick and uncooperative.

"Now? Babe, it's after midnight and pouring." Elisabeth worked her belt free and pulled down Stacey's sodden jeans, her underwear.

"Tomorrow," Stacey mumbled. "First thing. The book needs an ending."

"Fine." Elisabeth's new tone was different, but also very familiar. This one was cold and commanding. The conversation was over. She was naked, lying back on the bed propped on her elbows. "Come here, baby."

She did. And as she began dutifully kissing her way up Elisabeth's long legs, Stacey had to force herself not to glance at the mound of papers on the other bed. Stryker's work seemed to lounge there as if watching and grading her performance, waiting impatiently for the overdue return of her ministrations. Stacey went on worshiping the idol currently spread before her all the more passionately, willing herself not to think of Stryker or his stories. She would not tally the many, many hours she'd spent tenderly and tirelessly venerating those pages, adoring them. What she'd done to earn them.

No, she thought, it was not the same thing. Not at all.

Unsettling as the content was, Stacey hadn't been disturbed by the regular letters and parcels. Only their sudden cessation bothered her.

In the time between the arrival of Stryker's last missive and the police, who'd come to speak with Stacey in relation to his disappearance, having found her name and the address of the Nashville condo where she lived with Elisabeth prominently displayed among the remnants of her former teacher's abandoned apartment, she'd told herself she didn't care if he ever wrote again. She'd told Elisabeth too, and thought she'd meant it.

But at every opportunity, Stacey found herself secretly pouring through the large box of letters and notebooks, already beginning to arrange the makeshift manuscript he'd entrusted to her.

Stryker sometimes sent just a few pages, occasionally full legal pads. Some of his ongoing epic was typed, but the latter installments were written by hand, an increasingly illegible scrawl. Those pages were stained, smeared with dirt, as if maybe he were living outdoors or had been digging and could not be bothered to wash.

The language itself got more erratic as well. What began as a series of treatises on layers of the Earth, cave systems, the mythology of various famed underground civilizations and their depictions in so-called "subterranean fiction," had slowly mutated into bizarre nonsensical tales full of fantastic characters and hidden cities beneath the world of man. Some were quasi-political screeds about reptilian humanoids, ancient astronauts, and chaos *magick* (he was adamant about the alternative spelling). But there was a pattern, Stacey believed, a logical sequence to the writings. There was a story here, if only she could assemble the pieces.

When she'd hesitantly handed over the collection to the police temporarily, asking far too many times when it would be returned, Elisabeth had berated her for keeping it at all. The thing between Stacey and Striker was confusing and had nothing to do with her, and thus Elisabeth could not abide it. Stacey didn't blame her for not understanding. Elisabeth wasn't much of a reader. She'd only known Stryker as a teacher, as a man. And that, to Stacey, was the same as not knowing him at all.

Though mainstream success had eluded him, Kane "Stalk & Slash" Stryker was an original, as unforgettable physically as he was talented. There was no reason he shouldn't have achieved greater fame as an author, no reason except his own problematic predilections and a habit of alienating anyone in a position to aid his career.

Well over six feet tall, he was broad and beefy with long fiery red hair and the beard of a mad Russian monk. His eyes were the comfy blue of perfectly faded jeans and he had a way of training them on you that made the world go fuzzy at the edges, like you were standing on top of a tall building looking down. By the time Stacey met him, Stryker was a popular faculty member around the Knoxville campus, where he was engaged part-time as a teacher of freshman Earth Science and full-time as an emptier of whiskey bottles.

His prose was likewise distinctive.

Stryker had a knack, which served him well as he came of age artistically during the paperback boom of the 1970s and '80s, for recreating the best of what readers loved about the work of better authors. His speculative tales sold regularly, and a few were truly great, appearing in anthologies and magazines and even garnering some awards. His cosmic horrors were as eldritch and unspeakable as Lovecraft's. His violence was dramatic and epic as Howard's. He could conjure the same creeping dread as Poe, slather on awe and wonder pure as Bradbury.

But two things were crucially detrimental to his work, even beyond his famously difficult temperament.

First was an obvious and uncomfortable sense of malice. It's a given in the world of dark fantasy that bad things happen to good people; the universe is a harsh place at best. But in Stryker's stories, the reader couldn't help but sense a perverse glee. The author seemed to genuinely enjoy the sufferings he described, to be going out of his way to ensure the grimmest possible ending. For female characters especially, Stryker's mind was a dangerous and often degrading place.

Such pessimism was tolerable enough in small samples. It was even sometimes seen as bold (several of his stories were ultimately anthologized in definitive collections of new American staples) but cumulatively proved too much for even the most cynical readers.

Also hindering his writing was an abiding obsession with the underworld—subterranean societies of ancient pre-human races, strange creatures prowling the tunnels of a hollow Earth—which forced its way into far too many of his stories, regardless of subject or genre.

It's not uncommon for writers to take inspiration from the proverbial day job, and Stryker, who trained and worked as a geologist before turning to writing professionally, certainly had the scientific knowledge from which to draw it. But his relentless returning to the subject quickly exhausted editors and most readers alike. His work was published less frequently, then not at all, and Stryker was ultimately forced to take up teaching.

He'd had fans though. One of them was a Pensacola plumber. Looking to flee a failing business and marriage, he'd left his wife and child, a daughter, behind when he moved west with a waitress. The girl was little then, but years later, upon reaching an age where she naturally began to wonder about her absent father, she found a large footlocker full of the man's belongings in the attic of the small home where she lived with her mother and a revolving cast of boyfriends, unrelated uncles, and "special friends."

In it, young Stacey discovered a treasure trove of forbidden pleasures. Videos with graphic covers and sensational titles like *Night of the Living Dead* and *The Hills Have Eyes*. Half a pint of Jim Beam, the smell of which alone made her head whirl. A stack of dog-eared girlie magazines, which she'd been immediately, helplessly fascinated by. She'd thumbed through them when her mother was out or asleep, goggling at centerfolds, heart going a mile a minute and flushed with equal parts excitement and fear.

Most important of all, though, were the books: battered yellowed paperbacks by Lovecraft, Matheson, King, Dick, and Ellison. Plus nearly a dozen multi-author collections, in all of which the first page of the story by Kane Stryker had been folded down. Clearly, he'd been a favorite of her mysterious father.

Stacey read and reread those stories, imaging the man who'd enjoyed them and the man who wrote them. The two soon formed a vague singular figure in her mind's eye as she slowly embraced the harsh but pragmatic worldview of the stories and, in a way, fell in love.

Did the presence of Stryker's name on the faculty register sway her decision to attend the school? Stacey sometimes wondered.

Later, after everything that happened, she wondered a lot.

Inexplicably, the cemetery was located on a small hill behind Corrington Manor, just beyond the collapsed remnants of a once-grand pavilion. No doubt it had been the site of many fine weddings and concerts in the inn's bygone days of glory. Now, it just seemed as if the crumbling rot of the ancient graveyard was spreading beyond its rusty fence like some infection of neglect.

The rain had slowed to a drizzle when they made the trek, tired and moody (and, at least in Stacey's case, hungover) in the wan light of midmorning. Bypassing the low moss-covered markers, Stacey walked through the tall wet grass and immediately began investigating the names on the ten or twelve mausoleums in the rear.

She knew it right away by the name on the tarnished plaque: *Harvest.* That surname appeared regularly in Stryker's Frankensteinian masterpiece. Once, as the author of a fictional reference book. Another time, it was an explorer who supposedly vanished while searching for a way to access Stryker's imagined subterranean city, a place as realized as Bierce's Carcosa or Lovecraft's R'lyeh—a lesser Atlantis, sunk in dirt instead of sea.

The door of the moldering crypt was stuck tight. Stacey strained to open it. Behind her, Elisabeth whined, "Are you kidding me?"

Turning, her thick hair hanging heavy and wet, head pounding with last night's overindulgence, Stacey said, "The sooner you help, the sooner we're done. Now come here, baby."

She did. And, straining together, the women were able to drag the door open wide enough. The escaping air was shockingly cold and smelled of rot and mold. Just inside, beyond the reach of the weak daylight, all was stifling shadows.

From a pocket, Stacey took out her cell phone and activated a flashlight app. Leaning in through the doorway, she directed the beam forward—and saw it swallowed up by the utter blackness of the large hole in the tomb's brick floor.

The hangover gave way like a suddenly smashed window as her eyes followed the first three of a set of rough stairs leading down into the pit.

She smiled.

The accusations came in rapid succession. Six women reported Stryker for a laundry list of inappropriate behaviors and sexual harassments. The youngest was a sophomore who, just the year before, was a student in the last Earth Science class Stryker would ever teach. The oldest had already graduated, part of the same class as Stacey and Elisabeth.

His behavior had become erratic enough by then that school officials would have taken any excuse to legally oust Stryker, and this proved more than sufficient. He was at first temporarily suspended while the investigation was conducted, but everyone knew that was a formality.

Then, after he disappeared, it was a moot point entirely.

Stacey was saddened by the news, but less than stunned. She'd known Stryker well enough to long suspect such a revelation, or something similar, was inevitable. Though he never acted untoward or aggressive with her personally, during several of their longer late-night talk sessions, when he'd consumed even more whiskey than usual, Stacey saw a queer light enter his eyes as he looked her over. A strange smile appeared on his face and his voice got flat and cold—and then she'd been afraid.

But he had not wanted her like that. No, Stacey was something else, something even more precious: she was an audience. Not that it really mattered what he wanted her for, because by then she'd come too far to be skittish regardless of the man's intentions.

Salinger had Joyce Maynard.

Howard had Novalyne Price.

They'd begun meeting toward the end of her freshman year, at Stacey's suggestion. He seemed genuinely amused that a student—"and such a pretty one at that," he'd said through a smirk—knew his writing. Soon, he was inviting her to his apartment.

He'd shown her his books, an impressive library of equal parts pulp paperbacks and pristine first editions, and taught her the difference between rye and bourbon (though she never acquired a taste for either).

She'd gotten him to try sushi and introduced him to Netflix (though he distrusted both).

He'd lectured her endlessly about the untold history of fabled underworld civilizations and the devolved pre-humans living there; about what he called "entrance points," gateways disguised as cemeteries by their surface-dwelling acolytes, and the sweeping, encyclopedic tome he intended to write.

She'd kept copious notes of it all, even managing a few surreptitious audio recordings with her phone, already sketching outlines in her mind.

Kerouac had Edie Parker.

Brautigan had his daughter.

It was all coming together just fine. Whether Stryker eventually went out by booze or bad behavior, it didn't matter. Naughty boys make nice subjects. Then the selfish bastard went and vanished.

Hemingway had, well, everyone who ever knew him.

And Stryker, God help him, had her.

Regarding his disappearance, Stacey was merely intrigued...until the writings began arriving. That proved an unexpected (but not unwelcome) additional chapter. But still, enough was enough. What the book really needed now was an ending, one way or another. There was work for her yet to do.

So resolved, she descended.

Stacey and Elisabeth made their way carefully downward, led by the unseen leashes of ambition and obstinacy, respectively. The stairs devolved into a dangerously smooth clay floor on which their wet sneakers slipped easily. The smothering dark closed in, and the glow of the open crypt door grew small and distant behind them until finally it was swallowed completely. The cell phone light cut a slim path through the blackness.

Eventually, the ground leveled and they found themselves in what felt like a much larger space, though they could see neither ceiling nor walls in the darkness that surrounded them. A faint greenish light was emitted by a furry growth of strange mold that blanketed patches of the rocky floor. As her eyes adjusted, Stacey heard a man's guttural moan.

"Behold," he gasped, "I am vindicated."

She directed the light forward and saw him at last. Stryker was naked, seated on an immense chair made of rocks and bones. Something small and grub-white squatted between his knees, its bald head bobbing fervently. At the feel of the light, it sprang around to face them. Elisabeth screamed, shrill and piercing in the vast cavern.

The dwarf was skeletal, its leathery albino hide completely hairless. Huge milky eyes stared at them hatefully as the pink rosebud of its mouth bloomed, gaping impossibly wide to expose rings of needle teeth spiraling down its gullet.

It wailed at the light. The sound was appalling, and Stacey put her hands desperately over her ears until Stryker, his half-hard cock still dripping, stood and clapped his hands once. The thing fell instantly silent.

"I don't believe it," Elisabeth babbled. "Not real. Oh my god."

"No," Stryker said, reclaiming his seat. A ghoulish king in his Wagnerian throne. "Not a god. Merely one of the fallen. True rulers of Earth, driven by our ancestors down into the dark. Just as I, too, was cast from the *Paradiso* of cultural renown and academia's ivory tower to the pit of *Inferno*. But see, here I am exalted. It's truly better to reign in Hell, etcetera, etcetera."

The awful white creature growled and glared. Stacey saw two others lying on the floor beside Stryker's seat, both with enormous swollen bellies that seemed to throb and squirm.

"The children of the kingdom," Stryker said, eyes following her light. He reached out and petted one of the creatures on the head. It gave a low purr. "Imminent progeny of the new messiah."

In the darkness, Stacey heard the eager shifting of unseen masses.

"I've been walking up and down in the Earth." Stryker spoke thoughtfully, as if back in the classroom again. "All new dynasties are built on the crushed corpses of lesser gods. The world of the surface is weak. And our predecessors, first masters of the planet, are eager to return. Eager, but unprepared. Their ranks are sickly. I promised them vengeance. I promised them glory. I promised..."

"What did you promise?" Stacey heard herself ask, mentally recording every detail, memorizing everything. A good student still.

"Fresh mates." Stryker's face was carved by a scythe-smile. "New mothers to breed tomorrow's conquering horde. Sweet surface flesh to ravage. I promised them you, my most apt pupil. I never dared hope you'd arrive...*escorted.*"

Figures were becoming distinct in the blackness beyond. Shuffling, scampering, scuttling things of monstrous dimensions. Stryker cackled. He was thinner, almost sickly, Stacey thought, as if these things were not so much worshiping as devouring him. His long hair and beard were falling out in ragged patches, and his bony body was caked with filth. The green fungus light made his formerly brilliant eyes look desolate. Elisabeth was talking somewhere miles away and tugging at her arm. Stacey felt herself dragged backward a step.

The denizens of the dark were closing in, more visible now. Long fingers outstretched, their breathing quickened with mounting anticipation. Her taut and youthful flesh recalled in their collective unconscious the warmth of the sun, the caress of the breeze—the thrill of power. It was all true, what their strange new leader said. He'd descended to save them, to remind them their rightful place was to rule. They had been wronged. Displaced kings, they reached to possess this, their first new subject—the first of many.

Stryker said, "I knew you'd come. My own King James, translator of the new Good Book, here now to be the first martyr of the dawning age. I'll make you a saint."

Stacey pulled away from Elisabeth's hold and said, "I'll make you a counteroffer."

She whirled around and drove her fist hard as she could into Elisabeth's stomach, then brought a knee up into her chest as she doubled over. The blonde collapsed, gasping, eyes wide with surprise and dawning terror.

Stacey looked down on her crumpled centerfold, yet another lesser god, and said, "I told you not to come."

It was a good day for razing idols.

Tomorrow, Stacey would be her own acolyte.

She ran on alone. An infernal chorus of squeals and shrieks followed as she scrambled back up the tunnel, damp shoes slipping and her hands clawing for purchase, frantically moving toward the tiny faraway patch of light high above.

A touch fell—tenderly, almost—onto her calf. Stacey kicked out with her other foot in mad desperation and felt the meaty give of flesh and bone through her shoe. As she climbed, from far behind she heard someone screaming her name in a raw, inhuman voice. But her primeval will to survive roared more loudly in her mind, blocking out the sound and the pain of her gashed knees and torn-off fingernails and thoughts of anything but bringing the light closer. She moved forward relentlessly, without thinking, the way a rabbit outruns a fox.

But in a tiny secure place inside, somewhere deep beneath the thrashing primitive beast-her that knew already she would see the sun again—that she would breathe fresh air and live, goddammit, live!—crouched the calculating student.

Salinger had Joyce Maynard.
Kerouac had Edie Parker.

Let Stryker stew down there in the dark, she thought, brooding and lording over his newfound audience. Let him, like some abominable ginger Jesus, threaten an eventual righteous second coming. He would be years preparing for it, if he came through at all. Perhaps he would even prove more reliable than that other supposed redeemer, but there was time either way. Plenty of time to get it all written down.

A novel, Stacey mused. A metafictional horror novel based on the unsolved disappearance and bizarre final writings of an eccentric and controversial master of the genre, written by his former student and confidant.

His lover, maybe? That angle would sell better...

What's the difference between Dharma and Dianetics? Only a matter of time. She had it now, all the makings of a myth. The new Necronomicon.

Hemingway had everyone who ever knew him.
Stryker had her.
And the book, at last, had an ending.

Even as the ground rose into stairs beneath her feet and the light above grew larger, in that small quiet place inside, Stacey began composing her masterwork's first sentence.

Luciano Marano

For Karl Edward Wagner: Something special for the Last Wolf, from a thankful fan.

Shotgun Sunset

Maybe today.

Before the sun rises and the woman wakes, Papa comes, lifts me from the dark. We sit in the quiet until birds sing and night fades like a boxer's old bruises. He kisses me, searches for words. The good strong words, his life's work. They don't come anymore.

I'm a double-barreled beauty of flawless design. Like one of the man's own sentences in the bygone glory days. And when he asks, I'll kiss him back. I love him enough.

Ketchum's no Key West though, not even in July. It's summertime outside, but winter in his heart. He's a lifetime from Havana, Pamplona, Tanzania, and knows he'll never return. There are no more good fights. No more pretty girls or nights of glory. The Paris Ritz, Floridita, so many names gone from his mind now, like everything else.

Hands shaking, he cries over blank pages. Because worse than losing those other things is the growing certainty the words have left him too. The last time really was the last.

But it will happen, I'm sure.

Once more, at least.

Then he'll hold me and say, *Now, old friend, it's your turn to work.*

I'll do my best for him. The shy boy from Oak Park. Wounded romantic. Mean macho king. Patron saint of pompous party animals. The world's best bad dad. America's last swashbuckler. The sickly geezer sobbing when he thinks his wife cannot hear. I'll do it for her, too, the one still asleep upstairs. And all the others who believed in the words. The man. The myth. Everyone who needs this particular story to end as well as possible.

This place, it's as good a dying ground as any, I think. He's seen better—in Africa, Europe, Cuba—and always walked away. But all men go into the grave alone. Some whimper, some roar. And Papa? He's a lion and a hunter. Marlin and angler. Bull and matador. A battered brawler with spine enough for one final round before he takes me up and punctuates his last sentence.

Maybe today.

Different already. Steady hands. Clear eyes. He writes slowly...

One. Word. At. A. Time.

Faster now. He stands, sparring. Just a short note, but enough. The sun's rising. It sets on everything, but it also rises. Go ahead, ask him. Oh yes, it does.

Probably, he says, lips against me, *it should have been done years ago. Now, show Papa you love him.*

I kiss his closed eyes. True love headlong at 2,500 feet per second. We fall together and the floor is cold. Death's not just for the afternoon, but isn't it pretty to think so?

How else would you have it? That's what all the wannabes never understood. Flannel-clad poseurs stroking barrels, but too gutless to ever pull a trigger. Scruffy scribblers filling notebooks with nonsense. It takes balls *and* brains. See all the brains it took? Proof's on the page, people. And the floor. And the walls. Everywhere you look, he left a mark.

A man bleeds for everything worth having. Sometimes a little, sometimes a lot. Immortality ain't cheap. Someday they'll understand, but will anybody really care?

Maybe tomorrow things will be different.

Maybe.

Gobble

Twilight found us crouched in place, waiting.

A fence topped with razor wire towered ahead of us, and beyond that lay a wide field, tall grass swaying gently in the evening breeze. On the far side was a house, dark and empty. There was also a barn, shuttered and locked for the day, and three long industrial coops, each the size of a double-wide trailer. Ominous black rectangles with no windows.

The camouflage was excellent; to those who didn't know better, it would look like any other midsize poultry farm. Someone even thought to stick a folksy homemade WSU Cougars sign in the yard, right beside a larger, more professional one that proclaimed, *Shrike Birds—Best Breasts in the Business!*

Silently, we waited. Darkness fell on the world, sudden and heavy as a brick. There was no moon.

At Jack's signal, we moved through the hole Abdul cut in the fence. I paused, watching the action in night vision shades of green and gray on my video camera's LCD screen, trying not to focus too closely on Shaina's fantastic denim-clad backside as she slipped through the gap with enviable ease. Then I fumbled through myself and ran to catch up. This wasn't the most embarrassing thing I'd ever done to impress a girl (not even close), but it was definitely the most illegal.

Keeping low in the grass, we did our best to hurry across the open ground. If we would be caught, everyone agreed this was the most likely place.

Jack was in front—as usual—looking obnoxiously handsome and fit. The guy even took the time to gel and perfectly style his hair for the clandestine occasion.

Abdul followed him closely, the only one of us who moved like he knew what he was doing.

Shaina, her usually chaotic mane of dark dreadlocks tied together at the neck tonight, was next.

And yours truly brought up the rear, camera held in front of my face, already breathing hard and trying desperately not to trip. Maybe my checkered Vans were an unwise choice, but the only other shoes I owned were flip-flops.

We reached the first of several small outbuildings and huddled out of sight, eyeing the guard as he passed on his normal route at precisely the normal time. Although we'd observed the man going about his work through binoculars and camera lenses many times before, up close he was younger than I'd thought. It made me a little uneasy, truth be told. But Abdul raised his big Maglite without hesitation and brought it down onto the guard's head, crumpling the poor guy like a pile of laundry.

I couldn't help but wince, the reality of what we were doing hitting home at last.

Jack snapped his fingers, hissing, "Camera!"

And I swung the lens around to focus on him, dutifully playing my part. While Shaina and Abdul moved the guard behind the building and tied his hands and feet, Jack, oozing community theater charisma, looked into the lens and began his speech.

"It's July third, nearly midnight. We have exactly 29 minutes before the guard is expected to check in at the security shack. When he does not, the alarm will sound. By then we'll already be gone and the world will know the truth."

He paused to run a hand dramatically through his thick black hair.

"We have used the reduced staffing schedule of the holiday weekend to successfully infiltrate the highly secret Shrike Foods Test Farm, just outside Walla Walla, to uncover the unethical and illegal treatment countless turkeys are forced to endure as part of the company's so-called Poultry Improvement Project. The horrors of industrial meat processing are well known and extensively documented elsewhere, but the atrocities committed against the animals at this farm have been taken one step further with the aid of nefarious and unregulated science. Next, we will enter Coop Three, where a knowledgeable informant assured us the living results of Shrike Foods' unlawful genetic modification experiments are housed."

He slid an open hand across his throat and I paused the recording.

"All right," Jack said. "Let's do this."

I felt my attention drawn back to the guard. He was just about our age. I figured the guy had probably done a few stupid things of his own to impress girls. Probably had a mountain of his own student debt to worry about too.

"Wait," I said. "Shouldn't you, I don't know, maybe turn him over? Like onto his belly? I mean, he could puke and die or something, right?"

Shaina looked to Jack, who sighed and nodded at Abdul, who kicked the unconscious guard onto his stomach, eyeing me with undisguised loathing. A camera operator was a necessity of the moment, perhaps, but although my work would aid their cause (and Jack never tired of playing to the imagined audience I represented), I was not a true believer, so Abdul didn't bother to hide his feelings about me.

Abdul and I started on the wrong foot right away, and things hadn't gotten any better between us. Nervously, during one of the group's pre-raid planning sessions, I innocently asked the guy where he was from, just looking to make conversation.

"Afghanistan."

"Oh, which part? A big city or someplace in the country?"

Stupid. Even as the words left my mouth, I was embarrassed. What the hell did I know about Afghanistan? I couldn't find the place on a map if I had three days to search, and I sounded like a moron, even to myself. I remember very clearly how Abdul glared at me with unadulterated malice and said, "I am from the part where dreams are strongly discouraged. Why do you think I am here?"

I didn't know what dreams Abdul might have had aside from his outspoken desire to destroy those who would commodify another living thing, even such a seemingly simplistic creature as a turkey. I knew the dude was a vegetarian, but his true motives most likely originated in childhood, back in his harsh homeland. Or maybe during his military training. Somebody told me he'd earned his citizenship working with U.S. soldiers as a translator in the Middle East. But, honestly, I didn't really care about any of that.

And I wasn't overly concerned with whatever ultimate prize our fearless leader Jack wanted out of this dangerous and illegal endeavor either, except that it seemed to make Shaina happy to offer the douchebag my services as mission documentarian.

Shaina, though, she was another story altogether. I was *very* interested in everything about her.

The gorgeous biology major entered my life almost by accident when we'd been paired to give a presentation together in our history class. I was instantly in love, but Shaina was indifferent to even my most charming attempts at conversation and brushed off multiple invitations to go have coffee or see a movie.

Tagging along to a meeting of the animal rights group to which she belonged and spoke about often (founded by this guy named Jack, about whom she also spoke very often) seemed to endear me to her— albeit mildly. And when she asked for my help with the Shrike raid, I tried not to agree too quickly, later saving face with myself by reasoning that I had, in fact, needed a subject for my next student film anyway.

Secretly, I hoped my participation might elevate me somehow in Shaina's mind. But the mood tonight was much more serious than I expected (it was getting more serious all the time) and she'd barely glanced at me yet.

I tried once again to catch Shaina's eye, but Jack was already heading toward our ultimate target without looking back, and she was, as ever, hot on his heels. Abdul paused just long enough to jab a finger into my chest. "You are feeling better now, yes?"

"Yeah," I muttered, turning to follow. "I feel fantastic."

The main door of Coop Three was daunting, a thick metal slab fortified with several intimidating padlocks and one digital keypad. But Abdul apparently entertained even less regard for American security than he did for yours truly. The dour Arab quickly set about dismantling Shrike's fortifications with ease, using nothing more than a pair of slim silver tools taken from the pack tied around his waist. I thought I glimpsed something else in there, a tightly wrapped bundle of what dozens of movies and TV shows told me was dynamite, but I told myself that couldn't be right. Explosives weren't part of the plan.

In the time it took me to convince myself my eyes were wrong and frame the shot, the locks were on the ground, the keypad dark, and Abdul was swinging open the heavy door.

"This country," he slowly shook his head. "How is it you people controlled so much of the world for so many years?"

Stepping forward into the blackness, Jack paused, turned, and found the camera lens. With an obviously practiced grin that perfectly showed off his straight white teeth, he said, "Balls, my friend. That's how."

I could almost hear my eyes roll.

Inside the coop I could feel the size of the space, smell the dank soft earth beneath our shoes, the ripe and meaty stink of the birds. It was hot and moist like a greenhouse, and I instantly began to sweat. I heard the animals moving somewhere out of sight and panned with the camera. But even using night vision I was unable to pick out more than vague shapes. The rest of the team's flashlights impotently prodded the dark, revealing only the tiniest pieces of the room and not one glimpse of our quarry.

"Keep filming," Jack said. "There's supposed to be a bank of controls off to the left here. And a light switch."

Loud flapping, as if a dozen turkeys suddenly attempted and failed to fly in unison, exploded from somewhere to my right and I jumped, nearly dropping the camera. A series of sharp chirp-like calls sounded and were seemingly answered by other birds on the opposite side of the coop.

"Stop scaring the birds." Jack paused his search long enough to turn the flashlight accusingly onto me.

"I'm scaring *them*? Where the hell is that light switch?"

"Be quiet," Shaina whispered. "I hear something."

Jack said, "That's your boyfriend Ken Burns over there pissing his pants."

"I mean it," Shaina insisted. "There's something big moving around." She directed her light toward the unseen source of the rustling.

"Found it," Jack said. "Let there be light."

With a clank and hum, long strips of caged tubes running along the ceiling blazed to crimson life, bathing the room in a hellish glow, momentarily blinding us, but not before I caught a fleeting glimpse of the creatures.

It was deceptive at first because they were moving, but I quickly realized the young birds slowly surrounding us were very tall, heads rising nearly to my chest. And they were *really* fat. Great rolls of flesh piled atop two shaky legs that were mostly useless blubber jiggled above their small clawed feet.

Worst of all was their feathers.

They didn't have any.

What good are feathers to men obsessed with meat? An unfortunate extra step in the creatures' processing at last removed thanks to scientific refinement. The flesh of the birds was slick with clear viscous perspiration that stank of garlic and rancid butter. They were the bloodless pallor of things that spend their lives wriggling under rocks or squirming across the ocean floor. The complexion of life that exists wholly out of view of the sun.

"Oh my god," Shaina gasped. "What have they done?"

Jack was at my shoulder, reeking of Axe body spray and whispering excitedly, "Are you getting this?"

I could only nod, mouth agape, panning quickly across the circle of young turkeys. In some small part of my brain removed from the moment, I began formulating my Academy Award acceptance speech, imaging what color Shaina's gown might be.

The birds (dimly, I recalled from the team's research that a baby turkey was called a *poult*, not a chick) toddled closer in short bursts of eager, mincing steps before collapsing under their own top-heavy weight. Enormous breasts, meaty sacks like some hormonal teenage boy's favorite obscene cartoon, hung from their chests. Their eyes, vacant milky pools covered by thin layers of nearly translucent wrinkled skin, seemed somehow to both regard and simultaneously ignore us. They opened their colorless beaks as if tasting the air. Purplish worm-tongues flopped and twitched within.

Shaina jabbed her flashlight at the poult closest to her, but the beast did not flinch. "I think they're blind," she said. "Their eyes—if they're raised in darkness, they don't need eyes."

First one bird, then another, as if in response, opened their albino beaks and let loose a fresh chorus of the strange squawking calls. After each round, the birds all twitched their heads from side to side. With each session of the call-and-response, the nightmarish flock drew closer, inquisitively tightening their ranks around us, the strange new arrivals in their lightless world.

"It's some kind of sonar," Shaina said. "Like bats, I think. Everybody huddle together. We'll look bigger to them."

Abdul screamed. One young turkey had somehow snuck around behind him and gotten close enough to snap its beak closed on his arm. He wrenched free, blood pouring from the wound, and drew a long hunting knife.

Smelling the blood, the other poults began to squawk more excitedly, madly flapping their pudgy featherless wings and wobbling from foot to foot. It was like their bodies had been inflated from within, I thought. Pushed by chemicals and supplements to expand beyond anything nature would require. The noise quickly became unbearable in the echoing, cavernous space.

"Got it," I called out. "Let's go, I have enough."

"No!" Jack said. "We need a specimen."

"A what?"

"That was *not* the plan," Shaina said, swinging her flashlight back and forth in an attempt to keep the birds at bay.

"Forget the plan." Jack marched toward the nearing flock. "Nobody will believe the video by itself. They'll say it's some kind of stupid YouTube hoax. We're taking one of these birds with us. They can't ignore that."

The poult that bit Abdul was following him step for step as he retreated toward the open door, pecking at the drops of blood which fell to the dirt. Cradling the injured arm against his chest, Abdul slashed with his knife, but the turkey was not deterred. Two of its siblings followed and quickly encircled Abdul, who was now wounded and separated from the group.

Jack, too, had strayed into the midst of the featherless birds. He paused for a moment, but upon looking back and finding my camera lens dutifully fixed on him, as he'd so often demanded, he quickly masked his doubt and resumed pursuit. His face a perfect imitation of Hollywood hero intensity, Jack reached out and grabbed hold of a bird, which immediately began squawking in a new higher pitch.

Abdul shouted something in his own language and lunged, driving his knife into the poult nearest him. The blade sank with gruesome ease deep into the plump meat of its enormous breast and the animal collapsed, flailing its fat wings and emitting a strained wail.

The other turkeys took up the call even as they set upon their wounded sibling. Beaks pieced the downed bird, tearing it open so they could scarf the still-living animal's guts. The escaping wave of stink further incited the group, which quickly advanced on Jack, heads snaking out with unbelievable speed to remove his flesh in ragged patches. Each bite was tossed down a bird's throat with a swift jerk of their head before craning forward again to rip free another piece. Jack screamed and thrashed amidst the storm of ravenous mouths.

All of this I filmed, petrified as a fossil. I couldn't have found the camera's power button if I'd wanted to. Not that I was eager to actually *watch* what was happening. My eyes strayed desperately beyond the carnage to the far corner of the coop—and locked onto the flock's terrible matriarch.

Without feathers or feet, and completely eyeless, the enormous bird was a hulking mound of layered flesh rolls at least seven feet tall, whiter than a wedding cake's frosting. Its head topped a long snake-like neck, grazing the coop's ceiling. Gaping blisters freckled the monstrous bird, oozing more of the same pungent slime that coated its progeny.

Self-basting, I thought, hearing a bust of deranged laughter at the realization and understanding only afterward it came from my own mouth.

Feeling oddly numb, I focused on checking audio levels and redirected the camera so as to capture the creature's approach rather than scream. If I started screaming, I wasn't sure I'd be able to stop.

The mother bird pulled itself forward with long mutant appendages that may once have been wings. At their tips, black claws grasped the dirt. The long wrinkled stalk of its neck strained forward, giant beak yawning open impossibly wide. And from the Stygian depths of its gullet erupted a resounding call that seemed to rattle the walls.

Instantly, the poults abandoned their half-consumed sibling and retreated from what remained of Jack, scurrying to nuzzle their mother and cheep plaintively. Abdul was at the door, shouting for retreat. But Shaina was running to kneel beside Jack.

"I'm coming!" she shouted. "Hold on!"

His gurgling response might have been her name, but it was impossible to say for certain.

Shaina grabbed hold of Jack, trying valiantly to drag him to safety. But the enormous mother turkey had closed the distance between them with horrible speed. It loomed over Shaina, making inquisitive clucking and warbling sounds, twitching its massive head to and fro, inching closer with each call.

I heard myself squeal as a hand fell heavily onto my shoulder.

"Now," Abdul said. "We must leave."

He pulled me backward, still filming. I remember thinking that it was all for nothing if I didn't record what happened. We moved toward the door as Shaina turned, far too late, and lunged—only to be caught around the leg mid-jump by the hen's giant beak. I heard the distinct cracking of bones being crushed and Shaina screaming, but my eyes were already closed. Only the camera witnessed her demise.

Then I was outside again, back in the cool nighttime air, as Abdul slammed the door. Leaning against it, he gasped for breath, one arm dangling at his side, mutilated.

"What about the others?" I said. "We have to do something, right? What happens next?"

Abdul reached out with his good hand and tapped my camera. "That depends on you," he said. "They died for a cause in which they professed belief. If you wish, you can make Jack famous, as he always desired to be. And the girl, she also got what she wanted. She had his attention at the end."

I clutched my camera the way a drowning man holds anything that floats. My frazzled mind once again conjured a glitzy showbiz award ceremony. The low-cut dress of my date remained the same, although the part of its wearer would need to be recast. It was not a devastating revelation, and I smiled, turning the camera onto Abdul.

"And you? What do you want?"

From inside the building came a deafening squawk from the monster fowl. The crying of the poults became frantic as they pecked the door. From the pack tied around his waist, Abdul removed a small bundle of what definitely *was* dynamite and grinned.

"I wish to mark my first true Independence Day in this country with fireworks. And roasted turkey."

"I thought you were a vegetarian. And isn't that sort of thing against your religion anyway? What's Allah going to say?"

"I think perhaps even God would make an exception here." Abdul knocked lightly against the door, inciting a fresh round of cries from the birds inside. "And I never said I was going to eat them."

We managed to drag the guard, who'd returned to bleary semi-consciousness, a safe distance away before the explosion lit the night. Noise from the blast and the roar of hungry flames very nearly drowned out the anguished warbling of the dying monsters, the eerie sounds brought to us on the breeze as we rushed back across the field.

Long and brightly, the conflagration burned.

And the air smelled delicious.

Hāʻole

Stories like this reveal more about the teller than the subject, in my experience. But I'm an old man and despite everything that happened, I find I still miss my friend. So, as it appears he won't be stepping forth to regale any crowds with this, his last grand ghost story, in whatever time is left it falls to me to recount it for whoever cares. For whatever good it will do.

For myself, I just hope seeing the words on paper will give me some distance from the memory, like my camera in Vietnam. I was a photographer and, as Hollywood colorfully put it throughout the intervening years, *in the shit.* An overgrown boy eager for the chance to test myself against what I imagined would be the defining contest of my era.

Bullshit, of course. What did I know then about time?

But I'm not one of those still-in-Saigon burnouts you see in movies. On the rare occasion I examined the box of prints I keep in my closet, photos I took, they had no effect on me. I was removed, not only through the passage of time, but more importantly, by the lens and development process.

But now, after what happened to Gallagher, when I unpack those prints I'm shocked to find sensations coming back to me more vividly than ever—the suffocating wet heat of the jungle, sounds of choppers, gunfire, screams; the smell of mud, sweat, blood—as I recall the hell that brought me here, to paradise.

Hawaii is a strange place. A fascinating mix of scenic and seedy. Even as I stepped off the plane, three combat tours completed and discharge in hand, I knew I'd never leave. My ticket to the mainland went unclaimed. The ghost of a stillborn tomorrow that never had a chance.

Honolulu is the remotest city of its size in the world. The island of Oahu is barely thirty miles across, the capital city densely packed with the majority of the population. It's like we all washed up on the same strange shore and, faced with the vastness of the surrounding sky and ocean, the terror of our own inconsequentiality, huddled close together.

Hawaii has been invaded, conquered, stolen, and ravaged. The sunsets are beautiful works of art that tempt the most devout atheist. But behind the postcard-perfect tableaus and surfer chic, Elvis and Don Ho, air-conditioned buses hauling sunburnt tourists to sanitized excursions—beneath the pineapples, hula girls, and overpriced tchotchkes—is a mercurial land of war, strife, and death.

And ghosts too.

People think a place has to be ancient to be haunted, like those New England cemeteries and European castles supposedly so popular among the active deceased, but I think Hawaii, being young at least in a geological sense, has yet to be wrested completely from the gods. As every new volcanic eruption will attest, they don't seem to be done with it yet.

Spirits are part of life here. The ancient people knew it. Today's wiser residents believe it. Even the military accepted it (ask the old salts about the Shark Goddess of Pearl Harbor, if you doubt). And Gallagher, he made a great deal of money from it.

Honolulu is a city large enough to hold secrets and guard them well, but small enough so that anyone living here eventually meets everyone else. Stubborn rocks in a constantly rushing river of transients, visitors, and development, we tend to recognize one another.

So it was that I met Gregory Gallagher.

I'd managed to land a job as a photographer at the *Honolulu Daily Review*. It was weird, for a change, to be pointing my camera at people who would most likely still be alive next year. Otherwise, I spent my time playing tour guide to tourist girls. It was midnight on a Wednesday in August, and I was mourning the departure of a particularly friendly Texan named Becky in a Waikiki bar when, having finished one of his Hawaiian Horror walking tours (back when he actually hosted the tours himself, for he was not yet famous, having only published his first book a few months before), Gallagher—already known as the Ghost Guy—sauntered in for a nightcap.

The bartender placed a drink before him without so much as a nod. As we were both young, alone, and clearly no longer on active duty—though my hair was still short, I'd managed a respectable beard; he already sported the ponytail he'd keep for life—we began talking.

We discussed many things, as unaccompanied men in bars will do. We talked *around* Vietnam, as men often do (at least, those of us who were really there; those who'd been *in the shit*). Mostly, we talked about Hawaii. We were both *hā'ole*, after all—people not from there; a couple of white guys—who'd chosen to make a place for ourselves in this strange state. A sort of invasive species, you could say. We toasted the islands, and I got my first of many Gallagher lectures.

"By saying we had no breath, because the first Europeans here were unfamiliar with the traditional Polynesian greeting of *honi*, they were not only implying we were ignorant but that we literally had no spirit. No life inside us."

"I always just thought it meant we were pale," I said.

"It's slightly more than that. One Hawaiian scholar wrote the label originally indicated an alien creature having no relation to race. An outsider in every sense. One who does not conform to the mores of the group and is absolutely void of connection to the land."

It obsessed Gallagher, this concept of his own otherness. He'd been born and raised in Hawaii, the son of a prominent military doctor, and he'd never left the islands except when sent by Uncle Sam to spend a few bloody years aboard a brown-water gunboat.

But despite his insatiable appetite for Hawaiian history and folklore, and his respect for the customs and culture, he was never truly *of the tribe*, so to speak. I think part of him always hated the place for that.

It never bothered me, the melding and mixing of peoples and cultures being what drew me to the islands to begin with. But it's no stretch to see Gallagher's compulsive pursuit of Hawaiian legends and ghostly tales, his insistence on recording, documenting, and presenting them anew, as an attempt to make himself part of the narrative. To wrap himself up in the lore of this place for all time.

Now, I guess he finally succeeded.

Gallagher and I met regularly through the years as the landscape of the islands changed around us. Those meetings were, I think, like calibrating anchors for us both. Otherwise, we led very different lives. For him, I was a dose of reality, a sobering relief from specious specters and less-than-probable phantoms. And I found him compelling in his eccentricity and, despite myself, increasing fame.

Gallagher was a folklore instructor at a small university and already a well-known collector of ghost stories. People called him from all over the state to report possible hauntings and inexplicable occurrences, asking him to investigate. His office held an ever-growing collection of artifacts and evidence. The walls were plastered with photos of orbs and auras. His walking tours became more popular and he hired additional guides. His book was expanded and reprinted. He was frequently invited onto local television shows to discuss the subject and to pen guest articles for the newspaper.

I left the world of journalism, taking a job back in service of our beloved military industrial complex as a staff photographer at Pearl Harbor Naval Shipyard for exponentially more money. The hours, too, were more stable. Back then, there was a woman in my life: a fiancée who became my wife who became my ex-wife with shocking speed. Afterward, it was just easier to stay where I was, geographically and romantically.

A career's worth of grip-and-grin photos, promotion and retirement ceremonies, and industrial documentation passed unremarkably. The war pictures went into the aforementioned closet and I rarely thought of them.

Time is difficult for a single, childless man to measure. Women are more aware of its passage and effects, and children are living calendars. But for a man alone, the reality of his years comes home all at once and late in the game—a merciless ambush. Corny as it sounds, one day I looked in the mirror and found some geezer staring back.

Having witnessed the turning of the century, I elected finally to leave government service for the second time. The darkroom had given way to Photoshop, our interns kept looking younger, and I was glad to go. The island was different by then too, though some sordid secrets and occult corners still remained if one knew where to look. *How* to look.

I'd replaced the tourist girls of yesteryear with vacationing divorcees, enjoyed the company of a few friends and several hobbies. I liked to read, about ancient history in particular, and adored riding my Harley, which one can do almost every day in Hawaii. I was not unhappy. But a few days after retiring, I received an urgent e-mail from Gallagher, now a tenured professor and renowned author, which brought me to a bar in Waikiki for an impromptu catch-up.

"Frankly, I'm worried about you." Two sips into the third round, him looking at his watch like he was late for something, and Gallagher suddenly got serious. "I mean, honestly, what will you do with yourself?"

Raising my glass, I said, "You're pretty much looking at it."

He looked again at his watch. Even angry, he was handsome. A bookish movie star in thick spectacles, stylish tint of gray in his ponytail.

"You, my friend, are only happy when you're unhappy," Gallagher said. "First, it was your dirt-poor childhood back east, which you couldn't wait to escape. Then, Vietnam. Next, your lousy marriage. And a job you never once enjoyed. You love having something to hate. What do you have now?"

"Your lectures, apparently."

"Do you want your gift or not?"

"Can I have it now or must I answer your riddles three?"

"All you have to do is settle the tab and meet me out front." He fixed me with his about-to-tell-a-story look, the one I'd seen him use to mesmerize many crowds. "I'm being serious, Seth. We're already late."

Outside, rain had slicked the streets and sidewalks. The garish lights of downtown Honolulu were bleeding all over everything. Far off, on the Big Island, Kīlauea was grumbling, as evidenced by the noxious mix of fog and volcanic exhaust that weighted the cool November night.

We quickly found his Jeep and the pretty girl leaning against it. She was young, wearing a cheap convenience store sundress, slippers, and an enormous floppy hat. With a squeal, she threw her arms around Gallagher.

"Katie," he said, "sorry to have kept you waiting. This is Seth."

I was used to Gallagher's rotating cast of girlfriends, but in recent months he'd been exchanging them more frequently than usual. This one was new, clearly a tourist, and obviously very drunk. She hugged me enthusiastically, then offered Gallagher a silver flask from her small purse.

"I saved you some."

"Keep it," he said. "I'll drive. Hop in the back, darling, I need a word with Seth on the way."

Katie did, with a pout she probably imagined was cute.

"I'll follow you on my bike," I said.

Gallagher opened the driver's door and slid inside. "I'll run you back right after. Come on, we should hurry."

"I'd rather not leave it. How far are we going?"

"Not far."

I hesitated. Clearly, I remember the moment now and think of it often. How different things might have been.

Gallagher sped along the H-1, past Aiea and Pearl City, following the coast beyond Waianae and into Mākaha Valley, where it devolved from highway to slim rural road. Winding through the night, Gallagher made seemingly random turns. The houses got bigger, placed farther apart and back from the road. Many yards were gated. I do not think I could find the place again—not that I'm willing to try.

All the while, Gallagher talked. Occasionally, Katie would pass the flask from where she slumped in the back seat. Gallagher would hold it for a minute, but never actually take a drink, then pass it back. He didn't offer it to me.

"I've finally found it, Seth."

"What are you talking about? Where are we going?"

"It's the real thing this time. These people, I can't wait for you to meet them. They *know*. Do you see? They live the old ways and have been teaching them to me. It's exactly what we both need, my friend. Something to live for and believe in. Something *authentic*."

The flask came forward again, and Gallagher snatched it. "Thank you, darling. Doing okay back there?"

Katie mumbled something and burped.

"I think she's had too much, Gallagher."

"Nonsense. She's on vacation."

From the back seat, a weak little voice said, "The airport...he said...bought me a hat."

"I sure did." Gallagher handed back the flask. "Finish up, kiddo. Almost there now."

"Gallagher, really. I think—"

"Katie is from Salt Lake City," he continued. "She was on her way abroad for a... What did you call it, darling? A *mission*? Lovely. Anyway, after we met she decided she'd rather stay for a while, go to the beach, and think it over before spending more of her life in the service of a misogynistic sect founded by a failed treasure hunter. Her friends were not happy about it, which only proves the point I was very calmly making about intolerance before they started screaming. At least the cult of Christ has antiquity on their side, right? If one is going to be a believer, choose a doctrine old enough to have proven staying power, that's what I say."

Losing patience, I said, "What the hell are you talking about?"

"Just what I was discussing before, Seth. The source."

"Source of what?"

"Everything I've spent my life studying, they're just side effects. Symptoms of a condition I have thus far been unable to diagnose, to borrow some terminology from my father's profession."

Gallagher's father died years before and he almost never mentioned the man. His mother, who I gather he'd been very close with, succumbed to breast cancer when he was a teenager. I understood the men were then left to simmer in what became a lifelong stew of mutual tension and dislike. The old man disapproved of Gallagher's being unmarried, his decision to forgo medical school. But the casual way in which my friend now invoked the man—almost *fondly*—was odd.

We sped around a frighteningly sharp curve, tires shrieking.

"A few days before he died," Gallagher continued, oblivious, "he confided something to me. Throughout his career, my father resuscitated many people. They were clinically dead, Seth, and he punched into the ether and dragged them back to reality. He was not a religious man, but obviously he asked them about the experience. Scientific curiosity, he said. And each told him the same thing. Nothing happened. No tunnels. No lights. No voices. Not a single one floated over their body. There was only blackness."

"Shouldn't that have pleased you? You are a heavyweight skeptic."

"How right you are." His face broke into a strange grin that made me uncomfortable. I'd seen that smile before, looking back at me from photographs on the faces of doomed young men in a jungle far away, many years ago. It was the amusement of someone resigned to something terrible and unavoidable. A man sprinting gleefully toward the grave.

"I was pleased," he admitted. "Positively smug, in fact. Did I tell you I was with my father when he died?"

"You didn't."

Gallagher gunned the engine around another frightening curve. High walls of black trees loomed on either side of the road. Asphalt shone wetly in the headlights. In the back, Katie snored, dead to the world.

"He died screaming. Massive heart attack. Must have been agony."

"Jesus, I'm sorry."

Gallagher waved a hand dismissively. "No, it's *what* he screamed that has changed my life. See, all this time I never really believed, Seth. I was just playing along. Now, I finally know the truth. My father told it to me as his heart stopped and his body died around him."

I asked, of course.

"Just two words," Gallagher whispered. "*They lied.*"

Did Gallagher have a favorite legend?

Yes, in fact he did. Gallagher seemed to dwell upon one story most and returned to it often, especially late in our drinking sessions. It seemed never far from his mind, but the story wasn't any of those so popular with paying audiences—not the Menehune, the Nightmarchers, or stories of picking up Pele on the Pali.

In fact, he insisted it was no legend at all.

Though cannibalism was never practiced by the ancient Hawaiians (despite ugly rumors spread by European arrivals to the contrary) and was considered despicable, it was not entirely unheard of on the islands. Records tell of a giant—a great warrior chief, the historians called him—who came to Oahu sometime in the eighteenth century with rather zealous beliefs on the subject.

Where did he come from? Nobody knows. Some say he was driven from his homeland because of his awful tendencies. They say his native subjects at last tired of satisfying his voracious appetites and ran him off. Others say it was a simple political coup that forced his exile to Hawaii. What is known is he came alone, proffering no explanation. According to the stories, one morning the guy was just there, standing on a beach with the blazing sun rising behind him. He had no boat, no supplies. It was as if he'd simply walked out of the sea.

He was a brawler as deadly with his hands and teeth as any weapon, and stronger than four grown men. He preached a strict new gospel of *sacred violence* and immediately began gathering a following. He hosted orgies and mandated the ritual cannibalism of both fallen friend and vanquished foe alike, insisting such practices increased one's strength and extended life.

The ancient scholars called him *Ke-ali'i-ai-kanaka*, which I understand roughly translates as the King Who Eats Men.

Supposedly, he was from Fiji, or possibly a more distant island. But Gallagher insisted credible accounts exist which described him as looking more like a Viking, with long blonde hair, pale skin, and *startling eyes*. He might have been an albino, but Gallagher was convinced that *Aikanaka*, as the man was commonly known, was *hā'ole* in the true original sense—having no relation to race; an outsider who does not conform to the mores of the group.

Gallagher went even further, insisting the man had no connection to Earth at all.

The stories say Aikanaka established a small kingdom in the mountains of Wahiawa. Anyone who passed into his territory would be captured. Found worthy, they'd be offered the chance to join with Aikanaka's sect. Found wanting, they'd be devoured—roasted alive in an *imu*, placed upon an enormous flat stone, and carved up. Christian missionaries, so it was said, were his favorite meal.

Nobody knows how many souls met their end screaming for mercy in those hills before lowland warriors came at last, determined to slay the King Who Eats Men. The battle raged for days before Aikanaka, gravely wounded, was supposedly driven into the sea from a high cliff.

For decades afterward, stories persisted that the valley was haunted by the immortal spirit of Aikanaka, who'd eaten far too many souls to be killed. Even throughout the latter days of the twentieth century, some of the more superstitious old folks would lay the blame for every violent crime committed on the islands on the spirit of Aikanaka.

They said he now simply possessed new bodies so as to satisfy his terrible hunger.

Gallagher was talking again about the King Who Eats Men as he pulled into a long private drive and parked behind a row of empty cars.

The specifics of the mansion are vague in my mind, but every light inside was on, immense windows blazing brightly against the night. It should have been comforting, even cheery, but it was not. There was an eerie silence draped over the place. The wind ceased, even the fog thinned, as if unwilling to venture onto the property.

I retrieved the empty flask and sniffed the opening as Gallagher helped Katie out. The remnants smelled weirdly floral and much too sweet, not like any liquor I knew. Underneath was the vague hint of something rancid. My mind flashed on the image of savaged bodies rotting amidst pungent jungle flowers, but I saw it flat and glossy like in a photograph. My stomach roiled as we walked, Gallagher supporting the stumbling girl.

We circumnavigated the manor around to the backyard, which was enclosed by a fence of dark wood. The light from the windows mixed with the softer glow from strands of round paper lanterns hung above the gathering. I remember thinking it was some kind of student-faculty mixer because the ages of those assembled were so varied. Maybe sixty or seventy people were there, but it was hard to guess precisely because everyone seemed to be constantly in motion, as if preparing for something.

Two identical enormous men, shirtless and darkly tanned, their massive arms and chests adorned with bold tribal tattoos, were laying slabs of meat on a low grill above a glowing bed of coals. A pretty Chinese girl wearing a flower lei perched on a stool near a table cluttered with open wine bottles, gently strumming a guitar.

Katie was instantly swallowed up and carried away by a giggling horde of women. One of them, very pretty with silver hair, dark skin, and large eyes, took a swipe at Gallagher's shoulder, admonishing him for letting "the poor little dear" drink so much, before fleeing after the others.

They all knew him, waving and calling excitedly to Gallagher as he led me through the milling throng toward a row of coolers to pull slick bottles of Heineken from icy water.

Gallagher was quickly bombarded with hugs and handshakes from people clamoring around him, so I wandered away, trying to look casual despite my gnawing unease. My wife had been fond of entertaining, and she remarked often during our fleeting union that it was impossible to love a man so obviously happiest when alone. She left me without so much as a note. Had she considered that a kindness? Distracted by the surprise attack of yet another distasteful memory, I very nearly fell into the pool.

The underwater lights were off, making the water look black. It was outlined with blue tile set into cement and, much like the house, should have been inviting. Immediately, I thought it strange that nobody stood near the pool. They all gathered uncomfortably close together on the other side of the yard. I knelt to look closer—and saw the water really was black.

No, I realized, *it wasn't water at all.*

The pool was filled with inky sludge, something you might dredge up from the bottom of Pearl Harbor—the bottom of the Mariana Trench, for that matter. A primordial muck which had never before seen daylight. It stank too. The expected salty iodine of the sea, typical low-tide stink of the shore, and something else. Something musky and animal-like. Something rancid. I leaned closer.

The still surface was slick with shiny ribbons twirling and dancing across it. And beneath, for just a second, I thought I saw something. An even darker shape moving amidst the blackness. A small wave rolled across the brackish liquid, as if something big had turned over in the obsidian depths. I thought I could almost see it, something with too many limbs.

"Don't fall in." Gallagher was behind me, a fresh beer in each hand. His smile was too wide, voice too casual—a bad actor attempting something beyond his talent. "I don't think Marsha's had that cleaned in years. You'll probably catch leprosy or some damn thing. Come over here where it's safer."

I moved after him, trying to sound nonchalant. "You have to die of something, right?"

"Maybe." He passed me a bottle, eyes on the pool. "But not that."

The silver-haired woman approached again, beaming at Gallagher. "I like this one," she said. "I really do."

"Me too. Marsha, this is my friend Seth."

She was about a head shorter than me, and when Marsha clasped my shoulders I found myself looking down into her eyes, feeling as if I were falling.

"I'm so glad you're here, Seth. Gallagher's told us all about you."

Her face made me think of ship horns and train whistles sounding in places with names I could not pronounce. The world went gauzy at the edges as I stared. Then I came painfully back to reality, like a man waking after a drunken bender, as she turned her attention to Gallagher.

"Devout, you say?"

"On her way overseas in selfless service of Jesus Christ. Recently fallen. Very recently, in fact. I don't think the girl ever had a naughty thought until three days ago."

"Until she met you." Marsha's smile vanished. She jabbed a finger into his chest. "Tell the truth."

"Not a hand, Marsha, I swear." Gallagher looked a little scared. I'd never thought him capable of shame on the subject of his young female companions.

"It's not your hand I'm concerned about," Marsha said. "You promised. Not like last time."

Gallagher eyed the pool again, his face gone pale. "Not like the others. She's exactly right, just like I said."

"No, Gallagher." Marsha slapped his face. "Just like *I* said. She has to be pristine."

Beyond, the party continued. If anyone noticed what was happening, they gave no sign. The sound of guitar music drifted above the chattering and laughter. The smell of charred meat wafted through the air. I looked but could not find Katie among the shifting bodies.

Marsha whispered, "It's not me who will judge. And if she isn't right, if you've failed again, it's not me you will answer to."

She turned and disappeared into the crowd. I watched my friend struggle to collect himself, finally turning to me and waggling his eyebrows. "Saucy old dame. I always suspected she liked it rough."

"Gallagher, what is going on?"

"We'll know soon enough." His eyes strayed back to the swimming pool. "All I know is what I've seen. What my father said. Legends come from somewhere. The risk, I think, is worth...well, everything. It's worth everything if it's true."

"If what's true?"

"Don't you know?" Again the scary smile took over his face. "The second coming. The wolf that swallows the sun. The once and future king. It's the end of the world, good buddy, and I feel fine."

He went on, growing more excited. "And with strange aeons, who knows? Even death may die." Gallagher tittered and drained his beer. "More things in heaven and Earth and all that."

A scream silenced the revelers. I watched Katie being forced across the yard, struggling against a horde of women, their eyes blazing with mindless zeal. She was naked, a thick ring of colorful lei around her neck, strange symbols painted onto her flesh. I moved instinctively forward—still a young man of action, in my own mind, at least—and heard Gallagher say, "Don't, Seth. Please."

Like they'd been waiting for the chance, the Samoan brothers were on me, gigantic hands gripping my arms. I struggled about as effectively as the drugged girl did against the mob that bore her to the pool. Led by Marsha, they sang in a language I did not recognize.

The mire began to stir. It frothed and bubbled as if in anticipation while the crowd hefted Katie, bucking and twisting, eyes huge and rolled back in absolute panic, over their heads.

A collective exclamation of ecstasy was echoed at my sides by the brothers, whose hands still held me fast. And behind me, Gallagher sang out too, seemingly one of the tribe at last, having come through with his terrible membership fee.

I cannot be sure if I screamed. But Katie did. I will never forget that sound: the dying cry of a wounded animal cut dreadfully short by a splash as she struck the bubbling surface of the ooze and sank.

The brothers released me and hurried poolside to stand with the rest, all of them gazing fixedly into the still blackness. Gallagher's hand fell onto my shoulder. "I'm sorry. It's awful, I know. But it will work this time."

This time. How many girls had been offered to the thing I'd seen lurking in the depths of the pool? What was the horrible master these zealots hoped to appease?

The sound of splashing brought me back to the moment. Watching as the congregants pulled Katie from the water, I felt myself walking forward as they laid her onto the grass, wiping the symbols and black slime from her skin like nurses cleaning a newborn. Marsha cradled the girl's head in her lap, gently stroking her oily hair, smiling proudly.

The corners of Katie's mouth were split, like her lips had been forced open too wide. Her stomach was engorged, the skin stretched taught and slowly throbbing as if in time with her heartbeat. The level of the brackish fluid in the pool had lowered considerably.

As I approached, the unconscious girl began to cough. She sat up, spluttering out an immense gout of bloody sludge over her belly. Then she opened her eyes—their formerly cheerful blue had changed to a startling shade of gray so light as to be almost clear—to immediate applause.

In a deep rumbling voice, Katie spoke in a dialect that seemed impossibly old. The words of men who threw spears at the sun, I thought. Marsha's face streamed with tears, which Katie reached out one slime-covered finger to wipe away. She slowly licked her finger clean with a smile, then reached forward with both hands, roughly grabbed hold of Marsha's head, and kissed her.

Another explosive cheer went up from the crowd, but the kiss went on too long and Marsha began to struggle. When Katie moved her head, there was a wet ripping sound, and Marsha screamed as her tongue came away clenched tightly in the girl's bared teeth.

Katie stood, bulging stomach seeming to grow even as I watched. Her eyes roamed the gathering and fell onto me. I can still recall her smile, the way her eyes lit up like the first flash of dawn on the horizon. But those eyes darkened as she turned to Gallagher. She spat out the half-masticated tongue and spoke again, just two words, in English this time.

"They lied."

I was surprised to find I'd been retreating without thinking. I was beyond the crowd when Gallagher began to scream. As I turned to flee, I saw them reach for my friend with greedy hands and drag him to the ground. He begged for my help.

I ran around the house and—not bothering to stop at the car, for I was certain Gallagher had the keys—stumbled down the driveway until I reached the blackness beyond. All of the tropics seem alike in the dark, and Oahu was Vietnam and I was a young man again as I sprinted through the trees. Chased by the ghosts of ancient bullets, ears full of screams both fresh and faded, I ran until I collapsed and threw up, only then feeling my age. But I forced myself up again and ran on. I ran for my life.

That was nearly two weeks ago.

I found my way to the road and got a ride downtown from a passing car. My Harley was where I'd left it, wearing a necklace of flowers. Possibly they'd been tossed aside by some tourist, but I don't think so. The lei is a symbol of honor, celebration, and memorial. It's meant to convey the spirit of *aloha*, which of course means both hello and goodbye. I can't help but wonder which meaning they intended.

I went home to my silent house in Kāneʻohe and locked the doors and windows, drew the blinds. Retrieving my photos from the closet, I waited. Perusing the treacherous alleyways of memory, I awaited the return of the king.

Yesterday, I chanced walking to the store for supplies. I passed a young Chinese girl sitting on the sidewalk, strumming a guitar. She blew me a kiss.

Sometimes, the phone rings. I pick up, but nobody speaks. After a moment, a woman will begin to hum, always the same tune. It makes me think of wind rustling the branches of trees that were ancient when humans first walked erect. Waves crashing against shores that had yet to feel human feet. I think of vast sunken cities where the sun does not shine. The woman never speaks. I think maybe she can't anymore. Or maybe she just doesn't need to.

On the news today I saw they found Gallagher. It's a big story, a famous local author dying in such a grisly way. His remains were found in an empty pool in the yard of a private residence. The owner lives overseas, they said, and police have been unable to reach her. Identification required dental records, as the body had reportedly been badly burned and partially devoured.

A group of men are repaving the driveway of a house across the street. They've been there for days, but have made no progress. Supervising the effort are two identical brothers, both enormous and elaborately tattooed. When they spot me watching, they wave.

Today, I waved back.

———

Author's Note: *I lived in Hawaii for several years during the 2000s and return often to visit family and friends. Intentional superficial similarities exist in this story as a kind of playful homage between the character of Gallagher and actual Hawaii historian/folklorist Glen Grant, whose writing I've long enjoyed. Narrative liberties were similarly taken with actual Hawaiian geography and mythology for the sake of entertainment. Readers curious to learn more are directed to Grant's work* (Obake Files *and* The Secret Obake Casebook, *specifically).*

To Witness

Wesley beat the cops.

It happened sometimes, but not often. So he quickly pulled onto the shoulder, leaving his car running and the door open, grabbed his camera off the passenger seat, and leapt out, determined to make the most of his good fortune.

The drivers looked to actually still be inside their vehicles this time.

He needed this. The supposedly epic car fire his editor ordered him all the way out to Port Orchard to shoot had been a bust. A torrent of smelly smoke pouring from under the hood of an old VW van in a diner parking lot, some geriatric hippie insisting to the obviously annoyed firefighters, "It's never done anything like that before!"

Dumb luck found Wesley heading back downtown when word came over the portable scanner. It was the street name that cued him to how close he actually was: Magnificent Avenue. He used to buy weed from a guy who lived out that way, back when it was still illegal and everybody's parents had yet to start frequenting boutique dispensaries, casually throwing around words like *sativa* and *cannabinoids*, as if they were not eager to lock up even their own kids for enjoying the exact same thing just a few years ago.

Wesley couldn't afford anything in those new fancy shops and mostly stuck to beer these days, so he had no reason to be on Magnificent Avenue for some time. He'd always thought the name was somebody's lame joke, because there was certainly nothing *magnificent* about the road. It was just another heavily wooded strip of asphalt dotted with a few homes, neither stellar nor shabby, clinging almost desperately to the highway. Occupying that supremely passable patch of the Kitsap Peninsula that lay between the industrial epicenter of Bremerton and Gig Harbor, just across the county line. The absolute limits of the known universe, so far as his editor at the *Kitsap Daily Review* was concerned.

But he found it quickly enough: a three-car crash, pretty nasty one too. The smell—hot metal and rubber, burnt oil, and something else, something almost sugary that Wesley could never identify, no matter how many of these he shot and smelled—that strange mix so unique to serious car crashes, hung heavily in the air despite the chill breeze and drizzle. The drizzle which, he was practically certain, had caused the crash. It really was true, even here in the nearly ever-soggy Evergreen State: nobody could drive in the rain.

Wesley started working his way from wide to medium to close-up shots, moving nearer all the time, while listening for approaching sirens. They would let him stay because the law said they had to, but no cop would let him get this close again. Especially not with the bodies still there.

The Canon 5D Mark II was comfortingly solid in his hands, the resounding click of the shutter as familiar and automatic as his own heartbeat. As part of him saw only settings—f-stop, focal length, shutter speed—and compositions, the rest of his brain began to slowly take in what he was documenting.

There was a lot of blood.

It was smeared across one side of the cracked windshield of the blue Volvo sitting halfway off the road with both front doors open. A woman was lying in the grass near the passenger's side, one foot still up inside the car. Her other leg stuck out at a strange angle just below the knee, and a sharp point pressed outward from within her jeans. Wesley heard moaning, thought it likely coming from her. The front of the car, he could tell even from back where he stood, was completely crushed.

A stain of blood was also on the driver's window of the red pickup idling near the yellow centerline. A matted patch of dark hair was pressed against it, unmoving above the massive crater dented into the door and left front end.

That's where they'd come together. Not good for the pickup driver, Wesley mused, not good at all.

A third car, some black sedan parked slightly farther away on the shoulder, seemed undamaged. The windows were seriously tinted. Wesley wondered if the driver was a witness. Sitting inside, on the phone maybe? They could have been the one who called it in to the cops; somebody must have.

He noted the license plate had one of those twisted snake symbols on it, which meant the driver was a doctor or something medical. And there was a sticker with a blue cross symbol on the windshield, like a hospital parking pass. Could these people be so lucky?

Wesley absently snapped an artsy picture of the blood pooled on the road between the Volvo and pickup that would be way too subtle for the editor. It was being quickly thinned and spread by the rain and looked like watery ketchup. Probably, he thought, it was too much blood anyway. The editor would never use any of these pictures; too many angry emails and outraged Facebook comments were sure to follow.

Still, Wesley was now half of the floundering newspaper's two-person photography department left standing after the latest round of layoffs. And since Ancient Andy, who'd been at the paper since the industry moved on from stone tablets, had all the seniority in the world and showed no sign of retiring (or dying) and staff gigs for photojournalists were quickly becoming rarer than hens' teeth (one of Andy's favorite sayings), Wesley wasn't keen on returning to the office empty-handed.

Just shoot it already, he thought. Let the boss decide it's no good. Maybe he'd even man up and use one. Outrage was better than indifference. Clicks were clicks, and in the world of news reporting these days, it was the clicks that counted.

When he started out, eagerly rushing to chase every siren, Wesley probably would have felt something more at such a scene. Back when the newspaper's photo staff was robust and editors cared more about context than clicks (and he could still afford weed), he would have photographed something like this in an appropriately respectful manner. Now, countless collisions, fires, and too many miles of police tape to contemplate later, he simply considered how nice a contrast the reds of the truck and blood were against the mottled greens of the trees that lined the road, the gray of the overcast sky.

Pleased, he knelt so as to place the prone woman in the foreground, adjusting the aperture to throw the accident slightly out of focus behind her. It was front-page stuff. She was young and pretty, lying on her stomach with her eyes closed and the side of her face pressed almost gently into the wet grass. Straight hair, long and dark, was plastered to her forehead, but he could still see the ugly bruise there already darkening. Her lower lip was cut too, as if maybe she'd bitten it during the crash.

Wesley was wishing he'd grabbed his bag from the back seat, thinking of the great detail he could pull from her face with his 50-millimeter lens, when her eyes snapped open.

"He's eating her."

The woman's voice was a weak whisper, but startlingly focused. She was not confused, not babbling like so many others he'd photographed stumbling and staggering out of smashed machines. This woman knew exactly what she was saying.

Wesley snapped another picture, but it was no good now. She was moving, trying to get up, and it was ruining the shot. He began to tell her to lie back down and rest, that help was on the way, when he heard sirens growing louder in the distance and knew time was running out. So he left her there to crawl in the grass, stalked around the Volvo, and began shooting the truck. His phone buzzed in his back pocket—the telltale tone of a whip crack letting him know it was his editor—but Wesley ignored it.

Again, he worked from wide to medium to close-ups, moving around to the front of the truck, documenting the damage. The broken glass on the road. The dark hair pressed up against the bloody window.

The sirens crescendoed and began to fade, passing the exit and continuing down the highway. Were they lost? Wesley had found the accident easily enough. Where were they going? The rain soaked his hair and jacket, but was kept off the front of the 22-to-105-millimeter lens by the black tulip-style hood. The whip cracked once more, and again he ignored it, making his way around the front of the truck.

A man in dark blue coveralls was on all fours above the woman, who lay spread-eagle on the road with her mouth gaping open, wide eyes staring blankly into the falling rain. She was also young and pretty, and looked very much like the other woman; perhaps they were sisters? The blood on the Volvo's windshield had obviously come from the hideous gash on her forehead.

Listening, Wesley thought. This guy is *listening* to her heart, or maybe to her breathing. He's probably the doctor who owns that black car. The man's enormous bald head was down near the woman's face, eyes closed as if in concentration. He was smiling.

Of course he's listening, Wesley thought. What else would he be doing?

What else indeed?

Although, for just a moment, just the briefest flash of a second as he'd come around the truck, Wesley could have sworn that he was *licking* her.

Even as he recalled the other woman's disturbingly stoic report— *He's eating her*—Wesley robotically depressed the shutter button before realizing he'd meant to. The quick series of clicks was loud against the hush of the scene. The man glanced up and his grin widened. He was sickly pale and really, really fat. His bloated body strained against the jumpsuit as if barely contained, bulges of flesh shifting and pooling anew with each movement as he hefted himself to his feet.

"This one's just shuffled off," he said brightly, clapping his meaty hands together and rubbing them vigorously. "Always remarkable, isn't it, the way their lights just sort of blink out?"

Wesley's tongue stumbled over a response, his brain reeling to catch up (there was just no way he'd really been *licking* her, right?), and he mumbled, "Uh, I'm with the newspaper." He lifted his camera from around his neck and held it before him with both hands. "A photographer."

"Fantastic!" the fat man exclaimed. "Are you alone?"

"Excuse me?"

"What I mean is, do you work alone?" The man craned to look past him, down the street toward Wesley's idling car. "Is anybody else with you?" Three successive whip cracks sounded and the big man's face twitched.

"My editor." Wesley was whispering, but wasn't sure why.

"Oh?" The man's smile went on and on.

Wesley was noticing things now, his brain catching up to his eyes at last and registering unsettling hints that lighted one at a time, slowly at first, like stars coming out at dusk. He felt something enormous turn over in his guts, far beneath the fluttering disquiet in his chest. Interest, perhaps? Excitement? It had been so long since he'd felt either, Wesley could not be sure. This situation, he decided, merited a closer look.

The fat man was wearing little paper booties over his feet, like the kind workmen wear inside a client's house to protect the floor. They were quickly dissolving in the rain and blood. Through his dawning unease, Wesley noticed the name tag on the jumpsuit read simply *Patient.* He took a few tentative steps backward, the thing in his guts getting louder. No, it was definitely not excitement.

"I'm sorry," Wesley said.

"Not at all," the fat man beamed.

"The police," Wesley said. "I heard it on the scanner, they should be here."

"This one," the man tapped the dead girl with his foot, "did manage a call before she expired. But I imagine they're quite busy with that spot of trouble at the hospital. No doubt somebody stumbled upon it by now."

"At the hospital?"

"Yes, nasty business." The fat man shook his head gravely, but the smile did not falter.

The county's largest hospital was back in Bremerton, the way Wesley had been going when he heard the 911 dispatcher announce the crash. The sirens were coming this way though. They were going right past the accident and Wesley could not—

Puget Sound Psychiatric Hospital.

The thought hit him like a punch to the gut and the wind left his lungs. Wesley knew it wasn't too far away; only a few exits down the highway, in fact. In the same direction the sirens had been going. He recalled being sent to photograph the grand opening of the hospital (which Ancient Andy sneeringly called the *Funny Farm*) several years ago. He recalled the refined topiary arrangements outside, the lovely and calming shade of yellow the building had been painted. Anything so as to distract people from the noises coming from within, right?

"What's going on?"

A new voice dragged Wesley's attention back to the moment and he was alarmed to see how close the fat man had gotten. He could almost reach out and...

The woman standing by the now-open driver's door of the idling sedan waved cheerily. She was as thin as the man was fat, almost painfully so, and wearing a white lab coat, fully buttoned. Her skin was all but bleached of color, and her short dark hair had been cut very sloppily, the sort of thing a little girl might do with scissors.

"Who's your new friend, Kyle?"

Without looking away from Wesley, the fat man said, "This gentleman's a newspaper photographer, Kate. That's my sister."

"Oh, so good of you to stop," Kate said. "Is he alone?"

"Looks that way."

"Wonderful," Kate clapped her hands delightedly. "It's all my fault, I'm afraid. I just can't seem to keep straight in my mind which is the proper side to be driving on. The man in this wonderfully rustic little truck swerved to give me room and went right into the path of those lovely ladies in the cute blue thingy."

Kyle shrugged. "Women drivers, right?"

"Yeah." Wesley took another step back. "What can you do?"

As if their moves were part of some synchronized routine, Kyle took a large step forward and reached out. "Might I see your camera for a moment? I promise to be very careful. I'm thinking of buying one myself, you understand. Always been something of a firebug."

"Shutterbug," Wesley heard himself reply.

"Jitterbug?" Kate spoke from behind him and Wesley jumped. How had she come around the truck so quickly? It was raining even harder now, and he slipped as he turned, nearly falling.

"Litterbug?" She was close enough for Wesley to notice her glasses were too large for her head. They were crooked, and one lens was cracked.

"Bed bug." She laughed and clapped again. "Snug as a bug. In a rug. Wanna hug?"

She was wet enough for him to see she didn't appear to be wearing anything underneath the lab coat. The fabric glazed her skeletal body like paint. Her legs were bare below the end of it and so were her feet. She followed his gaze down and wiggled her unpainted toes.

"I just love going about barefoot," she said. "Don't you find it enjoyable to eschew shoes? Oh my, that's rather fun to say, isn't it? Eschew shoes. Try it, Kyle."

Gigantic hands clasped Wesley's shoulders and he felt waves of heat pouring off the enormous form just behind him.

"It was a truly terrible accident." Kyle's tongue probed Wesley's ear as he spoke. "Still, we probably wouldn't have stopped, being in a hurry such as we were, but it's Mother, you see? She gets so very hungry."

Wesley strained against the big man's grip, but one thick arm moved easily to snake around his waist and he felt himself lifted off the ground. The words for what he was feeling came to him then, silly as it was, and they came in Andy's cantankerous whine. He felt, as the old man would say, *like a goose just walked over your grave.*

Kate leaned forward and whispered, as if imparting a great secret. "Mumsie gets awful cranky when she hasn't had a nibble."

A familiar nostalgic feeling of weirdness washed over Wesley, making his fingers ache for a joint. That's what this was like, he thought, being way too high. And then he began to feel as if everything happening was always going to happen, that it was inevitable and maybe even important—maybe even *essential* for the continuation of what passed for reality—that it did. He was just a witness, after all, seeing these things as if through a window.

Calmly, he raised his camera and snapped a picture of Kate. Far behind her, something moved; something large and black. He zoomed in and saw the girl through the viewfinder, the one who'd crawled from the Volvo with a broken leg. She'd made astounding progress in her flight from the scene, having dragged herself nearly to his car, which was unlocked—the door was actually still open—the engine idling. She almost made it too.

The thing that sat atop her twitching form was like nothing Wesley had ever seen. It was a monster, a midnight-black beast with coarse hair, its enormous head lowered into an open crater of gore in the girl's stomach, slurping and chomping with unspeakable eagerness. It was truly *incredible.*

"Looks as if she's gone and helped herself," Kyle said, teeth nibbling Wesley's earlobe. "Mother's not one for restraint."

Wesley depressed the shutter button. Upon hearing the short burst of clicks, as if it knew he was looking at it, the thing went very still over what remained of the girl and then slowly raised its massive head. Strangely luminous yellow eyes, like alien suns seen through a magnifying glass held by some psychopathic child-god, blazed above its gaping maw of snow-white fangs, streaked pink now with blood. Little ragged bits of flesh dangled between them.

With something akin to what he thought must be terror, but not entirely unlike what he'd always imagined as being awe flooding his brain, Wesley pressed the button again, utterly unable to help himself.

The thing's tongues lolled out of its mouth, twin tips curling upward in a nightmarish approximation of an alluring beckon.

"That'll be a keeper," Kate said, then glanced wistfully over her shoulder. "We tried to tell them in the hospital. We tried to warn them that she'd eventually come to collect us."

Kyle hissed, "They said we were crazy."

"Legally insane," Kate agreed, reaching out to snatch Wesley's camera. His vision was suddenly forced into an expanded vista, one without the reassuring borders of the viewfinder. Bereft of their habitual burden, his hands hung limply before him, fingers twitching impotently. He did not notice.

The thing reared up on two impossibly thin legs, so much taller than it should have been, and began stalking toward them. The ground itself seemed to tremble. The trees cowered. Wesley's eyes would not close, not even to blink, and his ears were filled with a deafening otherworldly shredding he thought could only be the fabric of his own sanity giving way.

Faintly, he heard the incessant greedy clicking of his camera, a sound so far away as to be utterly inconsequential. A single rain drop in the ocean, it no longer registered in Wesley's suddenly widened world.

The terrible and wondrous thing before him grew even larger as it neared, until it was everything. Wesley saw in its eyes something he could not describe, but which he knew was exactly what he'd been looking for. In the screaming faces of the wounded and despondent, in the smiles of winners and tears of losers, in the shattered remains of every car crash, the smoldering leftovers of every house fire, he'd searched for it.

He felt the cool rain pelting his upturned face become warm and thick as it was replaced by drool, and the breeze became a blast of hot reeking breath, as he bore witness to its arrival.

Bleeding Black

I can still hear the screams as I plunged the needle into his face. Cries of rage and pain bouncing off the grimy tiles of the shower room, echoing above the huddle of struggling figures in orange jumpsuits.

There are no good people here, I thought, only degrees of evil. And I told myself that made it okay.

Given enough time, a more philosophical person might be able to find a lesson in what happened, some kind of moral. But to this day, when I can't stop myself from thinking about it—in the quiet between jobs, maybe, or during those long nights when sleep is impossible—what I remember most are the screams.

His.

"Please, no! Don't!"

Mine.

"Goddamnit, keep him still already!"

Those of the other men, the ones holding him down.

"Stick him! Come on, stick this motherfucker!"

The cigarette between my lips sent smoke into my eyes, making them water. I'd quit for good the next day, the smell too hopelessly entwined with that particular memory. Three months later, I'd be paroled. In six years, I'd own my own shop, win industry awards, and do this sort of thing for a living.

"Come on!"

The repurposed motor inside my jerry-rigged tattoo gun thrummed in my hand like a magic wand aching to conjure. Abra-fucking-cadabra, bitches. For my next trick, I'll need a volunteer…

"Stick him, Porter!"

And I did. My body became a machine. I turned off my brain, made myself see nothing but the line of the tattoo. A road leading me out of that room, beyond the prison walls, and into a better tomorrow. Blacktop shiny with blood, ink, and potential. No speed limits on that road. Not one single stop sign. I straddled Bradley's skinny chest, put the needle to his face, and etched into his forehead one word. A name.

KATHY

Blood ran into his eyes, wide with terror and startlingly blue. I remember them looking up at me, pleading. Sometimes I can feel Bradley's heart beating frantically against my leg, imagine his blood mixing with my ink, turning blacker than tar. Black as space without stars.

Mostly, though, it's the screams I remember.

And the feeling as my face began to ache and I realized I was smiling.

I was disposing of bloody paper towels and dirty needles, with the radio up loud, so I didn't hear the dead man come inside.

The black privacy curtain was drawn between my workstation and the front desk because today's final client was a Korean girl who wanted a kitty above her pussy. Some tattoo artists won't do work in that area, but I'll do whatever you want, wherever you want it. Two lessons I learned the hard way during a youth misspent going in and out of prison: 1. We must all live with the consequences of our decisions; and 2. How to sling ink. When I'm bearing down on the needle, skin is just skin. All I care about is the line ahead. A path as inexorable as the trajectory of a speeding bullet.

My assistant Arabella shouted goodbye when she left, locking the door and taking the cash to deposit on her way home, like usual. She was a promising young artist I met at group and hired about a year ago. Reminded me of myself, that girl, right down to the fading track marks.

I'd intended asking her to stick around while I finished with Korean Kitty, thinking it might make the client more comfortable. But since she'd lain right down and never once so much as looked up from her phone—which constantly *chirped* the most obnoxious sound throughout the entire fucking session—I figured she was plenty comfy and decided to save myself the OT. The shop wasn't doing *that* well.

The space next to mine was a travel agency specializing in tours of Italy, which was open just two days a week and, according to Arabella, was almost definitely a front for the mafia. Beyond that, the shabby unnamed strip mall was occupied by a teriyaki restaurant, a barber shop, and some kind of accounting office, all long since closed for the night. So I could crank the music without fear of complaint. And after hearing the door close behind Korean Kitty, I did. A mix of twangy-as-hell shitkicker tunes, which Arabella couldn't stand.

David Allen Coe was going strong but I was fading fast, and found myself ambushed by a surprise craving for cigarettes so intense I started imagining I could smell smoke.

Then, I actually saw it.

A thin trail of gray curling up from the other side of the cloth, snaking toward the ceiling. Pushing away the memories attached to that aroma, forcing myself to be angry instead of scared, I marched forward. This was my place, after all. The days of thinking like a convict were behind me. Here, I was in charge.

I said, "What the," as I whipped aside the curtain, fully intending to say, "fuck?" before being rendered speechless.

Korean Kitty was on the floor, obviously dead, her neck cut so deeply I could see a glint of bone among the wet red gore. She was splayed out in a pool of her own blood, like she might flap her arms and try to make an angel.

Of course her phone chirped just then. *Twice.*

Hunched on the couch in my reception area was an unbelievably ancient crone in a flowery house dress. She had a bouffant hairdo that never should have been allowed to outlive JFK, and a Pall Mall smoldering between two gnarled fingers. The pack rested within reach on a wheeled oxygen tank, from which dangled a plastic mask on a clear tube. She looked up at me with rheumy eyes made huge by thick glasses, each breath more strained.

And beside her sat the dead guy—or the guy who *should* have been dead, anyway. Bradley looked pretty alive though. Way too alive for my taste.

"Hello, Porter. Lovely to see you again."

A short, painfully skinny white guy with an uneven DIY buzzcut and the kind of teeth that came from a lifelong love of Mountain Dew and cigarettes, Bradley's face had a lot more ink than when we'd last crossed paths. But his eyes were the same shade of blue. They practically sparkled as he looked me over, seeming all the brighter for being surrounded by so much black and gray.

"I heard they carried you out of the pen a few years back, toes-up in a bag," I said. "Heard you took a tumble off your bunk with a strip of bedsheet tied around your neck."

"You heard right." He ran a finger down one cheek. "What do you think?"

Letters, shapes, and symbols done in various styles, by what seemed many different artists of varying skill, had been layered and melded together into a fantastically complex monochromatic piece covering nearly every inch of Bradley's face.

"It certainly makes you easier to look at. Being able to see less of you, I mean."

Bradley laughed, mouth open wide, bad teeth on full display. The lines and shapes spread across his face stretched into new, even stranger patterns.

I considered myself pretty hard to shock, but that face did the trick. And not just the fact it was still talking and smiling, despite so many reports to the contrary. A good chunk of my clients were alt-types or wannabes, and they favored weirdo occult stuff. I knew more about runes, sigils, and religious iconography than any dropout with a mail-order GED should. So I recognized right away there was some seriously dark and powerful stuff mixed into the mashup on Bradley's face. Most concerning were a pair of strange multi-pointed shapes on his eyelids, which I'd never even seen before. The whole thing obviously took a great deal of time and would have hurt very badly.

"Don't worry, Porter. I could never forget your contribution to this masterpiece—*unrequested* though it was. But it's cool, I have no hard feelings."

Bradley pulled out a long hunting knife, the blade still slick with Korean Kitty's blood, and dragged the edge across his skeletal forearm without flinching.

"In fact, I have no feelings at all."

The flesh parted easily, but the laceration didn't bleed, and it started healing immediately. In the time it took the old lady to affix her mask and suck down a noisy hit from the O2 tank, even the scar had vanished.

Bradley's smile made my balls retract in a hurry, but I couldn't stop myself from looking slowly upward, seeking out the word I knew to be written on his brow. Miles away, the stereo kept playing. Hank Snow was moving on, but I was stuck firmly in place, could barely even hear the music through the screams in my head.

I've tattooed faces, heads, boobs—I did a guy's dick one time—inside people's mouths, and even a few eyeballs. Never once have I refused a job. If you're over 18 and have the cash, I figure, hey, it's your body, right? But there was one tattoo, just one in all the years I'd been doing this, that I regretted. And there it was, staring back at me from the miraculously somehow not-dead guy's forehead.

Ghostly shrieks bounced off the walls of my skull.

Bradley placed a hand on the old woman's knee. With the other, he snatched the cigarette from her mouth and took a drag. "I've got a special job that requires a true artist like yourself."

The howling chorus grew louder.

"It's something of a repeat performance actually."

Try as he might, Bradley couldn't bury my work. No matter how many tattoos he'd piled on top of it, no matter how thick and dark the later stuff had been. The word I'd inked into Bradley's face all those years ago, as he cried and begged me to stop while being held down by a gang of furious felons, it was still lurking among the runes and sigils for all the world to see.

KATHY

The name of the little girl he raped and killed.

———

The story of my journey from abusing painkillers to thieving to support a junk habit is one so typical in this country it's practically a cliché. I was an awkward boy from a broke-ass broken home, artsy and sensitive: drew my own comics, played D&D, collected polyhedral dice, the whole bit. And I first started down the road of addiction using booze and drugs as confidence supplements. Let's just say I've made a lot of mistakes in my life—not that I'm making excuses (never forget Lesson 1).

Regarding Lesson 2, for that I have to thank Oakley.

The old guy claimed he was "half-Mexican, half-Omaha Indian, and 100% crook." A short brown-skinned dude with graying biker chops and textbook convict physique: pumped-up from the waist up, legs skinny as hell. When I met him, Oakley was slouching toward the end of a life sentence received for gunning down a guard during a robbery that went bad back when Bush was president—the first Bush, I mean.

His hands were getting shaky, the cumulative result of decades spent guzzling pruno and long-ago beatings catching up with him. Maybe he understood his time wasn't long and felt the need to pass on his knowledge. Or maybe there's something in a childless man of a certain age that drives him to seek a protégé, like whatever makes salmon swim upstream to mate and die. Most likely, though, the crafty old con just wanted to up his take by half. Because that was the deal we agreed to: his teaching me how to tattoo in return for half of whatever I got in payment for the work.

Oakley had been slinging ink in various prisons up and down the West Coast for longer than I'd been alive, reliably keeping himself in petty cash, prison wine, and, most importantly, protected. There's a kind of prestige that comes with being a good tattoo artist inside, and the old man slept like a baby no matter who his celly was.

I damn sure wanted that same peace of mind for myself. Not even sixty days into my longest stretch yet and I'd already experienced some interactions *of the sort I'd prefer to never think about again. Thirty-six months was feeling like a death sentence when Oakley came up to me in the dayroom to make his pitch.*

I was sketching in a yellow legal pad, trying to be invisible. My own ink back then was spotty, just a few pieces on my arms, all of it cheap flash. Although I'd designed tattoos for people before, it hadn't gone past paper. I'd never actually used a needle myself—not for tattooing anyway.

The old guy looked at my arms, then my drawing. "That's a pretty cool fucking dragon."

I mumbled thanks, although he'd have been hard pressed to comprehend it through my bruised jaw and loose teeth.

"I like dragons." Oakley sat down beside me, grinning. "In their caves, they always got lots of fucking money."

He swiped my pad and leafed through it, taking a moment to examine and consider each picture. Apparently satisfied, he said at last, "How about you, kid? You want to make some fucking money?"

A miracle by mistake.

An accidental wonder.

"Hurry up," Bradley said. "Get it finished."

And a less deserving beneficiary, I could not imagine.

"I'm going as fast as I can. This is a huge piece I would never attempt in one sitting, even on a healthier person. And in case you didn't notice, she's not doing so well. Your mom's skin can't take the abuse, see? It won't hold the ink."

Somewhere in the amalgamation of words and symbols on his face, hidden in the collage of jailhouse art for which he'd begged and bartered, amateurish experiments done by his own hand, and the vengeful branding by yours truly, Bradley was sporting a combination of shapes and lines that somehow allowed him to keep walking and talking, scheming and dreaming, without benefit of a heartbeat. His lungs held no air. His blood didn't flow. He was, by all conventional metrics, dead as a fucking doornail.

And yet...

"Like this," he'd said, pointing to his face. "Do it *exactly* like this."

And I did. I laid the old woman down and got to work behind the needle, telling myself skin was just skin, turning off my brain, and forcing my eyes to see nothing but the line of the tattoo.

The knife at my throat made it an easy decision.

Still, it was a rough start. Bradley's mother screamed as much as her decrepit lungs would allow. Her loving son held her down though, and soon enough her body gave out. Her protests were reduced to ragged gasps, which became weaker as the piece progressed.

Bradley stayed within arm's reach, playing with his knife between sharing cigarettes with the old woman, one after another, until the air was thick with smoke. He watched my every move and acted as a living reference at the same time.

Hours passed with unreal speed but, despite the circumstances, I managed to lose myself in the work, as usual. Eventually nothing more than hissing little breaths escaped the lady's tortured throat between increasingly infrequent pulls from the O2 tank. And I took advantage of the chance to do one eyelid while she was partially comatose. Inking that strange multi-pointed shape made me nervous. There was something genuinely evil about it.

As I finished, the old woman started mumbling to herself, words I didn't recognize spoken in a language I'd never heard. Maybe it was just the incoherent babbling of a sickly geriatric dying in agony, but it sounded eerily intentional.

"Her pulse is weak," I said, pinching her stick-thin wrist. "And her breathing isn't good either."

Bradley leaned in, our faces uncomfortably close above his mother's barely rising chest. The crone looked more corpse-like by the second, with only the angry raw beginnings of the tattoo giving her ash-gray flesh any color now. In her eyes I saw a desperate plea—and something else too. Behind the crimson spiderwebs of veins running through the whites, and the anguished distress blazing at their centers, something dark was flickering. A sinister kind of *presence* that I didn't like one bit.

"I never realized you were a doctor as well as a thieving junky." Bradley's lips pulled back from his terrible teeth. "And an entrepreneur besides! My stars, is there anything you can't do?"

"Please, Bradley, look at the woman. Show a little mercy, for fuck's sake. She obviously doesn't want this."

He lit a cigarette and blew the smoke into my face. "I don't recall either of us being overly concerned about the finer points of consent."

Ghostly screams echoed in my head as I met the old woman's gaze, saw the ominous *something* moving around toward the back of her eyes, and looked quickly away.

"I think your mom's going out of the picture."

Bradley reached out with his knife and tapped my cheek with the side of the blade. "Then work faster." His whispered breath stank of rotten meat and cigarettes. "Because if Mommy dies, you die."

A word came to mind as I returned the buzzing needle gun to the dying lady's face: *lich.* From the dusty vault of memory, the term, a holdover from my bygone dice-hoarding D&D-playing days, burst free. An undead creature reanimated by occult properties or necromancy. Not a ghost. Not a zombie. But something much worse. Something corporeal, intelligent, and deliberate.

Somehow, impossible as it seemed, Bradley was a genuine fucking revenant.

I didn't know exactly how it had happened. I didn't know how he'd fooled the guards and doctors, or what he'd been doing in the years since they gave his seemingly lifeless corpse to his mother at the prison morgue. But I damn sure knew what he wanted from me.

He wanted to make it happen again.

He wanted more time with his mommy.

The barter system takes on a heighted sense of importance in lockup, where possessions are strictly limited. And lots of guys doing time get religious about their bodies, pumping themselves up huge, covering their skin with the stories of their lives. They relive the past with every stick-and-poke, seeing with each jab of the makeshift needle those choices and mistakes that brought them to that place, got them locked in that cell. And they see the future too. The path forward.

As their flesh is penetrated to immortalize the name of a newborn they've yet to meet, lovers they hope to see again, or the savior they recently found, each man's body became his own map. And I became the cartographer of their souls. In accompanying so many on their journeys, I somehow eventually found my own way to the person I wanted to be.

Dope sent me to jail.

But the needle, that shit saved my life.

———

Dolly Parton was singing her heart out while Bradley spilled his guts.

It was a little after 4 a.m. I was exhausted, drenched with sweat, and fairly certain the old woman was dead. Leaning back in a chair with his feet up on a stack of boxes, Bradley, oblivious, playfully blew smoke rings toward the ceiling as he talked and I stalled, mixing ink, trying to decide my next move.

"I made a point to keep up with what you were doing. All the stories about you winning awards and opening this place, I made Mommy cut them out of the paper for me to keep." He tossed away the butt, barely missing a stack of paper towel packages. I vaguely wondered if my renters insurance was paid up.

"Of course, you can't take all the credit for this." Bradley waved a hand before his face. "I did quite a bit myself. I *had* to. Guys like me don't have many friends inside, as you well know. Finding anybody to cover up what you did to me, or even trade me the gear necessary to do it myself, that shit wasn't easy. I won't tell you what I had to do for those favors."

He stood and walked over to his mother. The old woman's eyes, thankfully, were still closed. But her breathing had basically stopped and her pulse was so weak that I couldn't feel it anymore. Maybe she was dead already and the tattoo's magic was working, keeping her body animated somehow. But when, exactly, had she passed on? I couldn't shake the feeling that by beginning the tattoo I'd started something, maybe even opened a kind of door. And there's no such thing as a one-way door. No telling what might have come from the other side to occupy this suddenly empty vessel.

"At first I couldn't understand what had happened to me," Bradley said. "I kept asking myself why I couldn't die. It made no sense! I must have slit my wrists every day for a month. And I hung myself at least a dozen times."

I raised the tattoo gun. "Maybe you're just super-duper special."

Ignoring me, Bradley stroked his mother's hair. "I tried doing this myself before we came looking for you. More than once I went out and found a test subject and tried to replicate the design on them. Despite my best efforts, they all died. And that's when I started thinking about you, Porter. And the good times we had together."

As I leaned over her, the old woman convulsed so intensely that her own flailing hands ripped the dress off her shoulder. I saw bruises on her bony neck, and on the sagging relic of her breast was a neat cluster of small circular burn scars, each about the size of a smoldering cigarette tip. Bradley followed my gaze and didn't even try to hide his smirk. I understood then he didn't really want to keep his mother around out of love—he just wasn't done torturing her yet.

"What happened to you wasn't my fault," I said. "I didn't have a choice."

Bradley drew the knife across his throat, opening a slit in the pale skin that should have gushed blood.

"You still don't." The cut healed as he spoke.

Maybe I didn't. And maybe Mommy Dearest deserved whatever she got. Men don't just wake up one day and become murderous pedophiles, do they? Or maybe we all simply become who we're meant to be in the end.

Regardless, no matter what kind of mother he might have had, Bradley was not exempt from Lesson 1.

And neither was I.

Finally, it seemed I knew what I was willing to live with.

"This is an important moment for you."

Oakley reclined in an infirmary bed, muscles wasting away, hooked up to an array of noisy machines. Beneath his ink, the skin was waxy yellow. A photo finish to see which gave out first: his heart or liver.

"But why me?" I sat on a stool beside him, nervously playing with the cigarette I'd been strictly ordered not to light up. "I'm not the only guy in here who slings ink."

"A sign of respect." Oakley shrugged. "They trust you."

"But I don't want to do it."

"Why? Not like he doesn't deserve it."

I tucked the cigarette behind my ear, then took it out again. "Sure, but I go before the board soon. I can't be getting in trouble now."

Oakley waved a trembling hand dismissively. "Piece of garbage raped a little girl—raped and strangled her. Even the guards hate this prick. You won't catch no shit, trust me."

A moment passed. We sat listening to the machines beep and hiss.

"Is there something else, kid?"

The words came out without thinking, before I even realized how true they were.

"You teaching me how to tattoo is the best thing that ever happened to me. When I'm working, I don't think about drugs anymore. Sometimes, it's like I'm not in prison at all. And I can see myself out there in the world really doing it, you know? Making something of my life. I think I could have my own shop someday. I could even hire kids like I used to be and teach them, help them. I really think I could do it."

He nodded. "I think so too."

"I don't want something so good to be mixed up with all this...bad."

Oakley pushed himself up straighter in the bed. "One of the boys here apparently knew that little girl's daddy on the outside, so it's going to happen. This kind of favor, they ain't really asking you, understand?"

"You're saying I got no choice?"

"Definitely not." Oakley's eyes shone bright as the edge of a blade. "You always got a choice, kid."

His smile was a jewel worthy of a dragon.

"All depends what you're willing to live with."

The needle found its mark, precisely where I'd left off. My body became a machine, but it was different somehow. This time, I couldn't turn off my brain.

There are no good people here, I thought, *only degrees of evil...*

When I'm bearing down on the needle, skin is just skin. All I care about is the line ahead. A path as inexorable as the trajectory of a speeding bullet. But the air in my shop was thick with smoke; my eyes began to water, and my head was full of screams.

In my hand, the tattoo gun thrummed like a magic wand aching to conjure...

I blinked hard, forcing myself to focus.

I made myself see nothing but the line of the tattoo...

...and changed course.

I rounded an angle, closed an open circle. A double line became a single, a pyramid became a diamond. The dead little girl's name looked up at me, pleading, and I forced myself to be angry instead of scared. This was my place, after all. The days of thinking like a convict were behind me. Here, I was in charge.

Bradley stood near the stereo, cigarette in the corner of his mouth. He'd ejected my country mix and was flipping through CDs. "How can you listen to this bull—"

His mother howled and went rigid.

I drew back quickly from the table as the old lady sat up and regarded me with new eyes, keen and bright, so darkly brown as to be almost black. An awful smile spread over her half-ruined face, and when she opened her mouth, many different voices came pouring out of her scream-ravaged throat. Each spoke the same words as before, in the same ancient dialect. A language I somehow knew was dead and buried long before the first humans came down from the trees.

Bradley pitched his cigarette and ran over. I saw the butt strike the black privacy curtain, tossing off sparks as it bounced.

"Mommy?" he yelled. "What did you do to her?"

The old woman leapt off the table and grabbed him, her thin frail body now possessed of impossible strength, and tossed him onto the floor. She leapt onto Bradley like a rabid beast, both of them screaming. Her mouth opened wide, far wider than should have been possible. I heard the bones of her jaw break and saw her tongue come snaking out, long and purple.

"I think my work speaks for itself."

Thick black smoke began filling the room, edging out the cigarette smog and momentarily clearing my head. I saw a trail of flames marching up the curtain. As mother and son began tearing chunks out of each other, I moved around the table, pausing only to grab the old woman's O2 tank and hurl it toward the growing fire on my way to the door.

In my hurry, I slipped in Korean Kitty's blood, falling on my ass so hard, the impact felt as if it flattened every vertebrae in my spine. I lay in the sticky puddle beside the girl and contemplated not moving anymore. It seemed easier, somehow, to stay put. She certainly wasn't complaining.

Then, I heard an all-too-familiar *chirping*.

Nope. Damned if I'd check out listening to that shit.

Bradley's screams and the infernal voices bellowing out of his mother grew louder as I found Korean Kitty's beloved phone in her pocket, then stumbled outside. I was halfway across the parking when my shop exploded.

The front windows shattered in a hailstorm of glass and the fire spread next door as, for the first time in my life, I voluntarily spoke to the police. And there I was, dutifully *staying on the line* as instructed by the 911 operator, when the flames reached the so-called travel agency.

That second, much larger, explosion was a surprise even to me.

Perhaps Arabella was right about that place, I thought. Hard to imagine anything in an ordinary office being so combustible. Distantly, I wondered if that might complicate my insurance claim.

Then, just for a moment, I saw two figures enrobed in flames and struggling together inside the conflagration. But after the roof collapsed, I told myself it was only my imagination. I sat down heavily on the asphalt, feeling the blood soaking my clothes become cold and my face begin to ache as I realized I'd been smiling.

I was smiling because the smoke filling my nostrils didn't make me think of anything in particular, not anymore.

And the only screams I heard where those of the approaching sirens.

Love Is a Ghost You See With Your Heart

Beliefs differ, as with everything else. But I've read extensively on the subject and understand many experts insist that places cannot be haunted, only people. We make our own ghosts, they say, or bring them along with us, trailing in our wake like shed skin cells or the lingering smell of some psychic perfume.

Nevertheless, I am certain it's our *house* that is haunted.

I don't believe I'd merit such attention from you, darling. Not even now, after everything that happened. No, it's certainly our house you're haunting. It took too long for us to find, and you loved it too much to let a little thing like death make you give it up. We paid more than we'd planned, but it was your dream house and you had to have it.

So I think you'd probably slam doors and rearrange furniture whether I still lived there or not.

Pretty good start, right?

Well, hold tight. It only gets creepier.

Scary stories are my favorite, both to read and to write. People don't often think of horror as being helpful, but I believe that's unfair. I believe it's through horror stories we come to know ourselves better.

I used to work primarily as a journalist, which means I wrote scary stories of a very different sort—but those horrors were never my fault. I didn't start the house fires. I didn't cause the car wrecks. I never even forced anybody to read the newspaper. But those scary stories were helpful (or at least informative).

Some people will always wonder at the appeal of horror fiction though. My wife, for instance. She can't stand the sensation of being afraid. She doesn't like rollercoasters and she hates scary movies. And she's not alone.

Why, these people ask, would you want to read or watch something fake that was made up just to frighten you?

But the horror genre has proven perpetually popular, even (and sometimes especially*) in times of uncertainty and turmoil. And I think that is because, in its own way, horror is reassuring.*

～～～

I don't mind the things you do, darling. Really, I don't. Break more plates, I'll clean up the mess and replace them. Shred the wallpaper if you like. I never cared for the pattern you picked. Tear all the books off the shelves and pile them in the center of the room. Most of them were yours anyway. Enjoy yourself, by all means. You always did prefer the company of books over me.

I hope you can see I've done my best to keep everything just like it was—the way you insisted it had to be. You always said I didn't listen, but see how carefully I replaced the books in the exact order you had them?

Remember how you used to get on my case about forgetting to clean the bathroom? Well, go ahead and make the walls bleed again, baby! I've got plenty of bleach and all the time in the world.

Did you notice that I kept your office exactly as you left it? Your desk and laptop, your notebooks and file cabinets bursting with new stories, they're all safe and sound in your favorite part of the house. The place where you spent countless hours making up fake adventures about imaginary people. People you loved more than me.

When I hear you clicking away on the keyboard now, it's almost like nothing has changed. I never saw you that much before.

～～～

Ah yes, the beloved tropes of the "haunted house" story—timeless, universal perfection. Horror gives us many such useful metaphors through which we can visualize, articulate, and confront our anxieties. We may never cure cancer, but we can sure stake the hell out of some vampires! Terrorists are legion and can strike anywhere, anytime. But Michael Myers is just one guy, and he only kills people in that one little Illinois town—and always on the same day!

Scary stories give us hope without sugarcoating the odds. They tell us everything isn't going to be okay—and that's okay! Horror allows for optimism, but never forgets where the exits are. And I think that makes the happy endings, when they do come around, all the more valuable.

There is a legend in the annals of pop culture that while filming The Shining, *Stanley Kubrick threw one of his famous tantrums and called Stephen King, in a rage, to vent. It was the middle of the night and King was hundreds of miles away, asleep. But he answered the phone and Kubrick reportedly said something like, "It's no good, Steve. This story isn't scary. If the hotel is haunted, there really are ghosts. If there really are ghosts, death is not the end. It's comforting."*

History doesn't tell us King's exact response—I like to imagine it was a variation of, "Who the hell is this?"—but Kubrick's theory got me thinking about ghosts being a comfort.

After all, a haunted house isn't such a bad place to live if your worst fear is being alone.

It's autumn again, finally, your favorite season.

Today, I raked the leaves that fell from the big tree in the backyard. The one you named for some Tolkien character (you're such a nerd!) and in which I carved our initials, which you said was a stupid thing to do. The one underneath which we once had a picnic on your favorite blanket. The one beside which, alone, in the middle of the night, I buried you.

Funny enough, it was a wedding present, the kitchen knife I used to finally touch your heart.

I used to worry that I wouldn't survive your absence. I tried taking an interest in your writing, but you said I was smothering you. I tried giving you space, but you said I was ignoring you. I tried to explain myself and you, half-present as always, nodded and pretended to hear, but really you were off somewhere in your head, busy with dreams of imaginary people and fake worlds.

But I had dreams too, darling. Smaller than yours, it's true. Less fantastic, maybe, but they were mine and they mattered and you never listened.

But I think you're listening now.

You heard me tell the police I didn't know where you were—and that night the bedroom windows shattered.

You heard me say I had no idea why your car was parked near the bridge, although, come to think of it, you were acting rather depressed lately—and from every faucet poured black sludge reeking of decay.

You heard me tell everyone there was no new work, that my brilliant and eccentric husband emptied his files and wiped his computer before he disappeared—and the water in my aquarium boiled, killing all the fish.

Yes, I think you're listening to me now.

Try to remember it's only a story, just something a writer made up. I wouldn't be doing my job if you weren't a little uneasy at this point. There are no such things as ghosts, probably. But I actually think writers are like ghosts to the people who love us and live with us—often more presence than present.

You feel us there, just out of sight or in the next room, but you can't communicate with us (especially not when we're on a deadline). And if you do catch a glimpse of us, sitting in the corner or while passing each other in the kitchen, it can be impossible to really reach us. Even when we're physically with you, part of us is always elsewhere. Back in the world we've invented, agonizing over our precious sentences, or standing off to the side, observing the moment and considering how we might best depict it on paper later.

I'm a lucky guy. My wife never begrudges me the time I spend alone, obsessing about people who don't exist and events that will never happen. She doesn't get mad when I'm distracted by a story idea and didn't hear what she just said. Twice. And lately I can't help but wonder, if the situation were reversed, if I could be half as kind and selfless. It keeps me up night, wondering about that. You see, I'm afraid that I know the answer.

We play with fear in order to master it. And fear, in turn, teaches us about ourselves. And while I like to think I'm a decent guy—does anybody ever really believe they're a bad person?—I work closely with fear every day, so I think I might know myself a little too well.

And I have doubts...

I still worry that I might not survive your absence. Lucky for me, you don't seem inclined to depart just yet.

Yes, I see you there, darling. And I caught a glimpse of you on the stairs the other day. You move much more quickly now, but not quickly enough to hide from me. I saw you lurking in the corner of the bedroom, too, just as I was torn from sleep after the windows shattered. I saw you behind me in the mirror when I wiped away the steam after my shower.

Muddy footprints in the hall. Cruel words—your words, I know them very well—scratched into my stomach. A dark figure in the shadow of our tree that seems to float just above the ground. A deathly pale hand sliding out from the pile of leaves, finger beckoning for me to come just a little bit closer. Kitchen knives impaled into the wall.

The phone rings constantly, but when I pick up there is never anybody there.

Maybe the experts are right and it's people who are haunted, not places. If that's true, maybe someday we'll get to haunt each other. Maybe we already are?

Or maybe I'm the one who's right. Years from now, a new family will live here and have picnics in the yard, rake the leaves, arrange their books on the shelves, and try their best to ignore the strange happenings.

Maybe they'll even joke about ghosts.

I think they'll tell jokes and learn to live with the things we do to each other or they'll move. Because it's our house, darling, and it always will be. And our house is haunted.

I wouldn't have it any other way.

Acknowledgments

This collection represents the culmination of nearly a decade of my professional life, and it would not have come to be without the encouragement and support I've been fortunate enough to receive from too many wonderful people to name here. That said, several key figures were especially instrumental in the lives of these particular stories, and I would be remiss not to thank Scarlett and the rest of the JournalStone team for taking a chance on this book; Serafine Hollowood for the exceptionally cool cover art; all the editors who first read, helped to refine, and ultimately published the stories within (especially C.M. Muller, who also provided the touching, pitch-perfect introduction); all the writers who gave me early feedback, commiserated, and contributed kind blurbs—dear friends and treasured colleagues, all; the valiant booksellers who made precious space for me on the shelves of their stores; the reviewers who enjoyed and said generous things about my work; the friends who were quick to order copies and attend events at which I appeared; the many patient bartenders who listened to me complain about events that never really happened and characters who technically don't exist (*see, I told you I was a writer!*); and Liane, my wife, best friend, and favorite person—a much better partner than I deserve. *Roll the window down and turn the radio up, baby. I believe we've still got a lot of miles to go together before this road runs out ...*

Publication History

"The Mythologization of Tymber Prescott in Five Selected Photos" first published *Nightscript Vol. 8* from Chthonic Matter, Oct. 2022; reprinted in *Brave New Weird: The Best New Weird Horror Vol. 1* from Tenebrous Press, Feb. 2023.

"Gargoyle Safari" is original to this collection.

"Struggle as You Will to Rise" first published *Chthonic Matter Quarterly,* Sept. 2024.

"'Till the Road Runs Out" first published *PseudoPod,* Aug. 2017; selected by *Signal Horizon* as one of the "Top 5 Best PseudoPod Episodes" of the year.

"Flickering Dusk of the Video God" first published *Monsters, Movies & Mayhem* from WordFire Press, July 2020.

"The Brief, Reluctant Retirement and Shocking Resurrection of Spooky Sophie" is original to this collection.

"Black Dog Blues" first published *The Half That You See* from Dark Ink, March 2021.

"My Eyes Are Closed to Your Light" first published *The Nightside Codex* from Silent Motorist Media, Aug. 2020.

"Shotgun Sunset" first published the author's blog, April 2021.

"Gobble" first published *Drew Blood's Dark Tales,* Dec. 2023.

"Hāʻole'" first published *Anterior Skies Vol. 1* from Strange Elf Press, May 2023.

"To Witness" first published *PseudoPod*, May 2021.

"Bleeding Black" first published *At The Edge of Darkness (Shotgun Honey Presents #6)* from Shotgun Honey, Oct. 2024.

"Love Is a Ghost You See With Your Heart" first published *Chthonic Matter Quarterly*, March 2023.

About the Author

Luciano Marano is an award-winning author, journalist, and photographer.

Born at a now defunct military base in Central America, he spent the majority of his youth in rural Western Pennsylvania before completing a 5-year enlistment in the U.S. Navy, where he served as a Mass Communication Specialist. Later, he received a BFA in Commercial Photography from a for-profit art school that no longer exists.

He is the author of the werewolf novella trilogy *The Ambush Moon Cycle* (Raven Tale Publishing), *Humbug* (Crystal Lake Publishing), and numerous works of short fiction appearing in anthologies such as *Year's Best Hardcore Horror* and *The Best New Weird Horror*, among others, as well as *Nightscript*, *PseudoPod*, *Chthonic Matter Quarterly*, and *Chilling Tales for Dark Nights*.

His written and photographic reporting has earned a number of industry accolades, and he was twice named a Feature Writer of the Year by the Washington Newspaper Publishers Association.

He resides near Seattle with his wife, Liane.

www.ingramcontent.com/pod-product-compliance
Lightning Source LLC
Chambersburg PA
CBHW020654260626
47157CB00008B/3033